THE PROPHET

CELIA AARON

The Prophet
Celia Aaron
Copyright © 2018 Celia Aaron

Cover art by Perfect Pear

Cover model Thom

Cover image by Wander Aguiar

Copy Editing by Spell Bound

CONTENTS

CHAPTER 1

DELILAH

*A*nother drop of water. I wince.

Drip, drip, drip.

Voices. Distant human sounds, but none that make sense. Especially when I know they aren't humans at all, but monsters.

Drip.

I know the water droplet is coming. I still flinch.

How long have I been here? There is no time in this place, none that I can measure. It has to have been at least a day, maybe two. I've pissed myself more times than I can count, but at least I haven't done the other thing... yet.

My hands and legs are bound, my head strapped to a board, a gag in my mouth that's connected to a taut chain. Or at least I think it is. I saw it before the light turned out and I was left in a blackness so complete that I wonder if I've been buried alive.

I can't turn my head. Perfectly positioned for the

1

dripping water. The back of my skull went numb a long time ago, and I wonder if it'll be flat when I get out of here. *If* I get out of here.

Drip.

"Fuck!" I scream against my gag, but the sound goes nowhere. Just like me. The only movement here is the constant splashing against the center of my forehead, rolling down my temples, and filling up my ears before rolling into my sweaty hair.

I clench my eyes shut, but when I do, I see *him*. Adam. He caught me and brought me to this torture chamber. I don't know what happened to the others who tried to escape, and I can't stop thinking about what's happening to me.

Drip.

Adam appears again, shoving me into the back of a white truck and holding me in an iron grip as some guy drove us through the property.

"They're going to hurt you." His whisper in my ear was surprisingly gentle even as he caged me with cruel ease. "But don't break for them. Promise me you won't. Don't let them tear you down to nothing." He sighed and pulled me even tighter. "I would have let you go, little lamb. If it were only me there in the woods. I would have let you go. Even though I would regret it, even though it would kill me with a million tiny cuts."

I shivered as the truck eased me toward an even darker fate. My voice was frozen in my throat, and I could barely process his words, much less respond.

"I'll be waiting." He kissed my hair as we stopped at a

nondescript cinderblock building without windows, and I later discovered, without hope. Adam stood at the doorway as someone grabbed me from behind and dragged me kicking and screaming into this fresh hell.

I've been here ever since. No food. No water, other than an errant splash every now and then from above that trickles past the ball gag—or maybe those are intentional. How long can a human go without water? Seems like something I should have learned in college. Maybe I did and then forgot.

I try to sleep, to let this nightmare place fade.

Drip.

Each cold splash jolts me awake.

Adam. I see his face. Different flashes each time consciousness slams back into me. When I first met him the night of the bonfire—the way his dark eyes drank me in and took far more of me than I ever intended to offer. The weight of him on top of me. The feeling of his lips against my skin. The hint of a man beneath the monster.

Drip.

But only a monster could have led me to this murky place. I was a fool to think he could be anything other than what he is—the Prophet's son. I'm only a sacrificial lamb to him. Nothing more. *"Where do you think you're going, little lamb?"* His voice slithers through my ears, and I strain to see into the blackness around me. But he's not here.

A scream rips through the air, then dies. Sounds of torment come and go like summer flies, landing and biting, then flitting away.

My thoughts race and trip, then fall headlong into despair. Flashes of memory catch like kindling in my mind. Eve was grabbed before I was. Susannah was trapped at the top of the fence, the barbed wire digging into her as she struggled. But maybe Sarah got away. And Chastity too. She'd almost made it to the top when Adam found me and pulled me away from freedom. A flame of hope leaps to life until... Drip. The orange light sputters out under the crushing weight of water.

I drift on a never-ending sea, sleep just over the next wave. But I can't get there. No matter how many times the languid ocean hushes me and promises me rest. It can't give it to me. Not here in the suffocating darkness with the ever-present drops of water. Who knew that something so simple could drive a person mad? A dry laugh sticks in my throat as I consider writing a strongly worded letter to Heavenly Ministries about their torture tactics. The chuckle turns into a cry, but I can't tell if the wetness in my eyes is tears or the drip, drip, drip.

Pulling against my bonds is useless, but I do it some-times, just to wake up my limbs a little. My upper arm aches where I dug out the tracker. But it feels off, as if they stitched it up. I can't remember what happened right after they dragged me in. I only remember this room, this empty black void.

I wonder if there's a brand new tracker in my arm now. Not that they need it. I'm in the Rectory, and I'll never get out.

More noises. Maybe footsteps? I strain toward the

sound, hoping for a reprieve. Maybe Adam's finally come to get me!

Something creaks and light filters in.

I blink over and over, my eyes stinging as they adjust to the not-so-total darkness.

"Bring her." A woman's voice.

Rough hands grip my wrists, and I sigh as the restraints loosen. My muscles ache as someone drags me into a sitting position. The Head Spinner, Grace, her face in shadow, unbinds my legs while someone else removes the gag. I lick my lips, my tongue like sandpaper. I wipe the water from my temples and ears, then suck it off my fingers. Nothing has ever tasted this sweet, I'm certain of it.

With a yank, I'm pulled from the table and dragged into a hallway, the cement floor cold and wet beneath my bare feet. Grace grabs my other arm, and the two Spinners march me past other rooms, the doors closed, mysteries behind them that I can't investigate. I can barely keep my head up, and my feet seem to have forgotten their job.

The Spinners don't mind, dragging me when I falter until we reach an open door at the end of the hall. They carry me inside and drop me in a heap at the feet of the Prophet. A threadbare rug separates me from the cold concrete floor, and the Prophet sits in a cushy chair, the fabric a deep crimson. I squint up at him. He gives me a benevolent smile and waves the Spinners away. They close the door when they exit.

"My dear child." He reaches down and tenderly pulls

my chin up so that I have to look him in the eye. "What have they done to you?" He inspects my face, then lets his gaze fall lower. A frown creeps into the creases by his mouth. "Grace!" His yell makes me jump.

The door opens behind me. "Yes, Prophet?"

"Did I not tell you to treat this tender child of God as a sacred female?" he barks.

"Yes, Prophet."

"Bring her water and food this instant!"

It's theater. It has to be. He's well aware of what's happening to me in this place. He put me here. He could free me if he wanted.

"Yes, Prophet." Only a few seconds pass before Grace sets a tray next to me on the worn rug. Fruit, water, little sandwiches cut into triangles—all of it there to tempt me. And it works. I can't stop myself from reaching for it, even though I know it's poisoned.

"You are blessed among my Maidens, Delilah. Chosen. Precious. Favored above all others." He strokes my hair as I take the glass of water and drink deeply. "Not too much." He places his hand at the base of the glass. "We don't want you to get sick. Try some of the grapes."

I take one. Knowing it's laced. Knowing this is all some big trick. But I'm so hungry that I don't care. My body won't let me care. I devour a handful of grapes, then drink more water, the Prophet petting my hair all the while.

"I know your heart, precious one. I know you would

never have tried to leave the safety of the Cloister if it weren't for the snake leading you astray."

I drink more and eat a sandwich. I feel like the sandwich has a rainbow inside it, but I can't see it, only feel its energy. With each bite, I'm filling up with color.

"She will be punished and cleansed until a serpent no longer dwells in her heart." He smiles down at me, and I can't help but return it.

"You're safe, Delilah. I will keep you from all harm. The Lord has given you to me as a holy gift, one I will cherish."

I nod, because what he's saying is true. The light that suffuses his fingertips tells me he is a true Prophet. And the food gives me light, too. And it's all because of him.

"Thank you, Prophet." I lay my head in his lap as he pets down my back.

"You are on the right path." He presses another grape into my mouth, his fingers lingering against my cracked lips. "The Lord is pleased with you."

"It's all because of you." The grapes seem to dance on the plate, vibrating from positive energy. I grab another handful, jealous of how they sway and glisten.

"I must go, my darling one." He stands, and I grab his hand. "But I'll return to check on you." Leaning down, he kisses my crown.

"Stay," I beg and try to grab his pants leg.

"Soon, my child. I'll see you again very soon." He walks out, taking the searing energy with him.

The light seems to dim once he's gone, and I want to

follow him, but I'm rooted to the spot. I don't know how long I stay there, thinking of him, before the door opens.

Grace is there with another Spinner, their batons raised.

My screams seem to come from someone else's mouth as I'm dragged back to the never-ending dark.

CHAPTER 2

ADAM

Three days. She's been in there for three whole days, and no one will tell me a goddamn thing.

"Are you listening to me, son?" My father snaps his lighter closed and takes a hard drag from his cigarette.

"Yes." I try to relax my shoulders and appear nonchalant. "The Maidens are getting back in line."

"They are." He lets the last word hang in the air. "But." It sounds like a shot. "We need to discuss Craig. As Sarah's Protector, he's the one to blame for this entire episode. The Maidens are being punished, but it's time for him to face the consequences."

Finally, my father and I agree on something. Craig is a fucking animal and deserves to be put down like one.

"What did you have in mind?" I have plenty of ideas.

"The whip isn't enough, but the cross is too severe." He raps his knuckles on the desk.

"The river?" Noah asks, his voice tentative as he suggests torture.

My father smiles. "I think that'll do just fine." He turns to me. "We also need to discuss your punishment, Adam."

I don't react. I assumed I'd be up for some more lashings. If a Maiden disobeys, and especially if she goes to the length of trying to escape, her Protector is punished. In my father's eyes, we aren't doing our jobs. The girls should be broken by now, with no spirit except one of service to the Prophet.

"Will I get the drowning treatment, too?" I hold his icy glare.

"At first, I thought the lashes would be the best thing for you." He takes another draw. "But then I realized you need a bit more."

"Bamboo under the nails? Maybe let rats gnaw at my fingers and toes?" I hope one of these is correct. Whatever he intends to do, I want it done to *me*. But the glint in his eye tells me that's not how this is going to go.

"Bring her!" His voice slices the air.

Castro pushes through the office doors, shoving my mother inside. Noah and I jump to our feet.

Noah starts, "Dad, you can't—"

"Sit the fuck down, Noah!" His bellow cows my brother, but not me.

I stare him down. "This doesn't concern her."

"Everything to do with you concerns *her*." My father snaps his fingers and my mother limps over to him, but gives me a pleading look as she goes. She doesn't want me to interfere. Just as always, she's trying to shield me. One broken leg and multiple bruises and scars have never stopped her from trying to keep Noah and me safe.

"Don't." I curl my fingers into fists and step toward the desk.

Steel presses into the base of my skull.

My father smirks. "If he moves, pull the trigger."

"Yes, sir." Castro pushes the muzzle harder against me and grabs my shoulder with his free hand, shoving me into the chair.

My fingernails dig into the skin of my palm. "Castro, I promise you. One day, I'm going to have your warm blood on my hands. And I can't fucking wait."

"We'll see." He's still cocky. But soon, I'll make sure he never takes another breath.

"Rachel, my love." My father grabs her hands and pulls her to him.

Noah squirms in his seat, and Castro kicks the leg of his chair. "Move and I'll pop you."

"Prophet." She doesn't meet his gaze.

"Have you missed me?"

"I miss my husband, yes." Her words are strong, even though he's tried so many times to break her spirit.

"Would you like to prove it?" He takes another drag and blows the smoke in her face.

"How?"

"If you are telling the truth then you won't be harmed. But if you aren't in perfect obedience, I'm afraid this is going to hurt." He grabs her arm and slides up the sleeve of her white shirt.

She doesn't move. When he presses the burning cigarette to the flesh on the underside of her arm, she makes a small sound, but swallows it.

Castro's grip tightens on my shoulder. Of all the things my father has done in his presence, *this* is what bothers him?

"Oh, Rachel." He pulls the cigarette away and tsks. "You were lying after all. You didn't miss me. You aren't in perfect obedience. That's why this hurts. But my darling—" he tries for a frown but can't quite get there, his glee at the thought of human carnage too great "—you know it hurts me far more than you."

Can I grab Castro's gun before he pulls the trigger? Would I be able to kill him, then my father without drawing any other Protectors? My mind works and works, desperate to solve the equation as my mother flinches. The smell of her scorching skin taints the air as my father marks her again and again. Noah white-knuckles the arms of his chair, and I can do nothing but watch.

I've known for years that I'd kill my father. But I didn't know how close that time was. The last time he tortured my mother, I was too young, too shocked to do anything about it. She still bears the limp from an untreated break. And when he destroyed Faith, I was too lost in grief to turn my rage outward. But this time is different. Now I know what I have to do—for my mother, for Noah, for Faith, and for Delilah.

And I will do it soon.

~

The Rectory is dark, and there's a guard stationed outside with an assault rifle. I prowl around in the nearby trees, all my senses attuned to that one dark building where Delilah suffers. Three days and nights of torment. Fuck.

I lean against an old pine as something skitters through the underbrush about ten yards away. The moon peeks from behind fast-moving clouds, then disappears again, taking its light with it.

Saving her isn't an option. Not with armed guards and everyone on high alert. The escape attempt—though not the first—was the only one that came so close to being successful. More men patrol the compound, and the Cloister is monitored even more heavily. There will be no more late night dashes for freedom. My father's fist is closing around this place, choking everyone inside under the love and guidance of the Prophet.

Headlights cut through the night, and I shift around the tree to remain hidden. A white Range Rover passes, then stops next to the Rectory. My father gets out and strides toward the entrance, the guard hurrying to open the door for him.

I can't be sure what my father does while he's here, but I can guess. More mind fucks, more drugs, more promises rolling off his tongue. I told Delilah not to break, but as I stare at the windowless cinderblock building, I wonder if she has any chance of staying whole. She's strong, but torture can crush anyone.

"Hey."

I turn and reach for my pistol.

"It's me." Noah creeps among the trees until he leans against a twisted oak to my right. "I figured you'd be out here somewhere."

Sliding my hand off my pistol grip, I return my gaze to the Rectory. "What are you doing here?" A memory of the last time we talked glides through my mind—how I was cruel to him because he still believed in our father.

"I just figured—" He sighs quietly. "I don't know. You seem sort of drawn to this Maiden. So I thought maybe you needed—"

"Thanks." I can't tell him that what I need most is to kill our father. But Noah's presence is welcome, if unexpected. "About what I said the other day—"

"Don't worry about it. And maybe you're right. After what he did to Mom, I don't know." His voice drops even lower. "I can still smell her skin burning."

"Me too." I bury the memory of her pain, but I remember the spot like a dog with a treasured bone. I'll dig it up later and use it to inflict damage on those who deserve it.

He peeks around his tree. "Is Dad in there?"

"Yeah."

"Shit."

The wind is still, the crystalline air stagnant and silent. Long minutes pass as we wait—for what, I don't know. She isn't coming out. Not until she's "ready," according to my father. I grind my teeth.

"Maybe they just do the regular sort of stuff in there?" Noah sounds far from certain.

"You mean light torture with a side of brainwashing?"

"Yeah, that." He shrugs.

"I don't think so."

He knows as well as I do that what happens in the Rectory makes the Cloister look like a Disney vacation.

"You think he's going to..." He swallows audibly.

"Claim her?" I want to say no, that he wouldn't do that because maybe he can still use her. Maybe she won't be sent to the Chapel or the Cathedral. She still has value as long as her body isn't too broken. I snort a dark laugh. Her body can't be broken—that would kill her value. But her mind must be utterly shattered, then put back together with the glue of my father's lies.

Noah shrugs. "He's only claimed one. Maybe he's going to be a little more careful this time."

"And not fuck them before sending them off to their assignments?" I pat my jacket pockets for a pack of cigarettes that hasn't been there for about five years. "He can't help himself. No way he'll let one go without sampling her."

"But maybe not yet. She could still be—"

"Shh." I grab his arm.

My father struts out of the Rectory and hops into the waiting SUV. When it takes off, Delilah's scream pierces the night.

It does something to me. Inside. As if I can feel her agony deep in my gut. I don't realize I'm running until Noah tackles me from behind, ramming me into the pine needles and undergrowth and hiding us from the headlights of the passing SUV.

"The fuck are you doing?" He rolls off me and sits up. "You want to get caught?"

She screams again, and my blood scrapes against my veins, urging me toward her.

"I want her out of there!" I climb to my feet as her cry dies off.

"No." He rises and grabs my arm. "You can't. If you even try it and Dad finds out—"

"Mom." I already know that she'll pay for whatever mistakes I make. Again. Running toward her still makes complete sense in the hollowed-out casket of my heart, but my head reminds me that Noah is right. If I step out of line again, our mother may pay an even dearer price than some charred flesh.

"Come on." He lets go, perhaps assured that I won't make a move. "Is this Maiden worth it?"

Yes. The word streaks through my mind like a bolt of lightning, but I don't dare say it aloud. Giving it breath would be acknowledging the weakness. "She's mine."

"She belongs to the Prophet." His voice gentles, but the barb still hits its mark.

He's right. Whatever connection I feel to Delilah will ultimately be severed—either by my actions or by my father's. That knowledge doesn't change a goddamn thing.

"Come on. Let's get out of here." He punches me lightly in the shoulder and jerks his chin toward home.

I reluctantly turn and follow him, though I leave far too many broken pieces of myself with Delilah, both of us suffering in our own dark abyss.

CHAPTER 3

DELILAH

*G*eorgia flies through the air, her golden curls streaming out behind her like flags of sun and happiness. Her laugh reminds me of hot days spent at her house playing in the back yard and racing each other around the neighborhood on our bikes. Her pink dress is one I've seen many times—girly and perfect, just like Georgia.

But this scene is off. The swing creaks as she kicks, each movement twisting something tighter into the branch above, digging deep into the oak's flesh, leaving room for bugs and rot.

A grownup Georgia turns to me, a pentagram carved into her forehead, blood trailing into her eyes. "Come and play."

I can't move. It's raining. Water drips down my hair and shakes the leaves above us as the sky roils from gray to black. It isn't summer. Not anymore.

She jumps from the swing and dashes around the

tree, her pink dress shredding away and revealing skin marred with cuts and burns, emblems of several ancient religions oozing blood down her tan body. "Let's play chase!"

"Don't go!" I struggle to follow her, but my limbs won't move. Tears roll down my cheeks as thunder rumbles overhead. "Come back, please."

"I miss you." Her voice floats on the wind as a tornado forms nearby, black dirt rising into a catastrophic funnel that whips across the landscape. "But I don't want you down here with me. Don't let them send you to this place." She dances out from behind the tree, her skin white, her eyes rolled back in her head.

I scream as she lurches closer, dirt in her hair, death leaking from her rotting pores.

"Don't let them send you here." Her voice is watery as the tornado approaches, the funnel even blacker than the sky.

Water pours onto me, and I sputter, awakening into a hint of light in the pitch darkness that has become my life.

"You're screaming like a banshee, Delilah." Grace's voice cuts through the haze of my dream, then she dumps another bucket of water on my shivering frame. "It's your sins. They eat at you." She walks around me, her fingernails trailing down my leg. "You don't belong here. That's why you tried to leave. Your sins urged you to go out into the world and be what you really are—a slut, a fallen piece of trash, nothing and no one. But here you are." She slithers closer. "Still in my care."

Drip.

I try to fight against her words, her poison, but she continues, "You are nothing more than a scrap of trash that desires nothing more than to spread your legs for whatever man or beast that might come along. You'd sell your disgusting body in a heartbeat. That's what animals like you are made for. Breeding. You have no other purpose." Her nails dig into my shoulder. "You were nothing before you joined the Cloister. But once you did, you became more than just a filthy sinner, you became blessed among women, a jewel of the Prophet, chosen by the Almighty to lead a righteous life in service. And what did you do? You acted like a slovenly whore. Leading Protector Newell into temptation and corrupting Adam with whatever lies fell from your forked tongue. You are lower than the serpent in the garden." Her warm breath fans across my cheek. "You disgust me, you disgust Adam, and you disgust the Prophet. You will die here for your sins and be cast into the darkest pit of hell."

A drip from above smashes against my forehead. And that's when I feel myself shatter. I scream and strain and fight, but I go nowhere. She's lying. I try to shake her tenterhooks free from my mind, but the barbs are in deep. I bite my gag and try to kick free. I barely move. The struggle ends quickly, when my last bit of energy fades. And suddenly, I know she's right. She's been right all along. I don't belong here. I am filthy. I've failed Georgia and myself. I am not worthy of the Cloister, and certainly not of the Prophet or his son.

"The only way to free yourself from your prison of

sin is to accept the Prophet." She leans next to my ear. "You must be in perfect obedience to him. Offer everything you are to him. Beg for forgiveness."

I can see it in my mind. Bending before the Prophet, offering him my body, my soul, my everything. And my heart finally seems to beat again.

Drip.

My fears fall away. This place is only temporary. A short stop on my way to salvation. The Prophet is the key.

I want to say yes, to beg to see him, but the gag prevents it.

Grace leaves, closing the door and entombing me in darkness.

The Prophet will save me. I thought that Adam cared about me. I was wrong. I thought I was here to find the truth about Georgia. Wrong again.

I'm here to serve the Prophet. Hot tears pour from my eyes as the truth settles inside me like a seed, sprouting and growing. The Prophet. He is my only love, my only light, and my salvation.

CHAPTER 4

ADAM

*A*fter another night of barely sleeping, I wake early as I hear Noah's footsteps echoing on the polished wood stairs. I sit up and rub my eyes, then glance at my alarm clock. Daybreak is in half an hour.

"Is Dad coming?" I ask as Noah walks in my bedroom door.

"Yeah."

"Fuck." I rise and stride to my bathroom, the polished marble reminding me of a crypt.

"Craig's already in the back of my car with Gray and Zion."

I stare at my haggard face in the mirror. "Does he know we're going to the river?"

"No, but he's shaking and stuttering. Probably thinks it's the cross."

"He might have preferred the cross when that cold water hits him." I pick out some jeans and a t-shirt. "You got the waders?"

"In the trunk." He sits on my bed and glances at the blanket on the floor. "You sleep?"

"Enough."

"So, that's a no."

I pull my white t-shirt over my head and grab my belt. The one I'd used on *her*. I have an instinct to press the leather against my cheek, hoping for some sort of phantom warmth or her scent.

"You okay?" Noah rises.

I glance at him. "Better than you are. You buttoned your shirt crooked."

He looks down and grins. "Well, shit."

"Fix it in the car." I walk past the door across from mine—the one I never open—and pound down the stairs, my hollow footsteps bouncing off the walls. The four bedroom house was meant for a family, the hardwood floors and luxurious furnishings perfect for one of my father's favored Protectors. Instead, he gave the house to me, to keep me close, to keep an iron grip on every move I make. Classy and classic, the home is far nicer than the ones I grew up in. And though there are no bars on the beveled windows, it's a prison all the same.

The brisk morning air hits me full force as I walk down the brick front steps, Noah at my side. White exhaust puffs from the black sedan waiting in my driveway.

"I'll drive. You fix your shirt." I slide into the driver's seat and cast a glance at the rearview. A ghostly-white Craig doesn't meet my gaze.

I would like to say I don't enjoy this. But Craig is a

vicious son-of-a-bitch, and he deserves every bit of what's coming to him. More, if I'm being honest. I find myself hurrying through the Compound, speeding toward Craig's chilly punishment. When we pass the clearing where three crosses are set deep in the Alabama clay, Craig lets out a low sigh of relief. I smile and gas it, almost getting some air over the next rise. Noah shoots me a worried look, but doesn't say anything.

We veer away from the main buildings and pass the guarded road that leads to the Cathedral, then head deeper into the woods. When the dark river emerges ahead of us, Craig makes a noise low in his throat. Fear permeates the air, and I flex my fingers. I'm ready.

I pull up to a gravel area at the water's edge. Boulders and mossy rocks appear along the edges of a wide pool with overhanging trees. In the day, the water is almost clear. But now, when the sun hasn't risen, it's gloomy and bottomless.

"Get him out." I glare at Zion in the rearview.

He and Gray jump at my words, then drag Craig from the car and slam the doors.

"Looks cold." Noah holds his hands over the warm vents. "I fucking hate this."

"Why?"

"It's just so... so..." He throws his hands up. "Why do *we* have to do it?"

I cock my head and study him. "So, you don't mind the fact that Craig is going to be drowned to within an inch of death, but you *do* mind that we're the ones who have to get our hands dirty?"

"When you say it like that, I sound like a psycho." He shrugs. "I mean, in a perfect world, no, Craig wouldn't be punished like this. But..."

"But what?"

"But he failed his Maiden, and he failed the Prophet."

I clench my eyes shut. "And here I was beginning to think you were finally getting over the hump of our father's bullshit."

"You saw the flames." He crosses his arms over his chest. "We both saw what he can do."

"We saw a parlor trick! And we were stupid kids!" I wonder if I can slap the belief out of him, just rear back and knock him senseless. But it won't work. If my father's taught me anything, it's that true believers will hold onto their blind faith no matter what. I grind my teeth. "He's just using you like he does everyone else, Noah. None of this is real. You aren't here because you believe. You're here because of what he'll do if we try to leave again."

"No." He shakes his head. "I may disagree with some of the stuff he does, especially when it comes to Mom, but he's the real deal, Adam. You have to know that. You *saw* it!"

"I don't know what I saw, and neither do you." I slam my hand on the steering wheel. "You have to snap out of it!"

A car pulls up, its tires crunching on the gravel. The driver steps out and opens my father's door as Noah and I fume. But this discussion is tabled now that Dad has shown up.

"Let's get the waders on." Noah opens his door and steps out.

I force my anger to recede and adopt a placid expression. My father doesn't need to see anything that goes on inside me. I've become good at hiding in plain sight.

Despite the façade, I can't help the eager way I pull on my waders and grab Craig for his date with oxygen deprivation. The water is frigid, chilling me through the thick rubber of the waders. Craig stiffens and shivers as we haul him into the pool.

His screams and cries for mercy are hidden by the black water as Noah and I shove him under. He kicks, splashing us, as my father intones, "For we were all baptized by one Spirit so as to form one body—whether Jews or Gentiles, slave or free—and we were all given the one Spirit to drink."

When he finally stops moving, we pull him up. I slam my open palm against his back, and he coughs up water, then takes a huge gulp of air.

"... and this water symbolizes baptism that now saves you also—not the removal of dirt from the body but the pledge of a clear conscience toward God." My father nods toward us.

We slam Craig beneath the glacial water, his struggles filling me with a rare sense of satisfaction. He didn't listen to his Maiden's cries for mercy. I saw her, the one with the dark hair and the bruises. The one who was screaming the night when Delilah fought with all her might to try and save her. Sarah, the one who led the escape attempt.

"Let him up, man." Noah shakes my shoulder.

I didn't notice Craig had gone slack again. We pull him out of the water, and I land blow after blow on his back until he coughs and sputters, then starts begging.

I grin and shove him back under.

Some parts of me—the worst—are the only ones I ever let show.

I walk up the slight rise to my father's house. Castro stands out back smoking a cigarette. He flicks the butt at me as I reach for the back door. Pausing, I do a quick calculus on whether I could kill him and get rid of his body before my father or anyone else asks questions.

"Problem, *pendejo*?" He taps the pistol strapped beneath his arm.

"Fuck you." I push inside the house and slam the door in his face, flipping the lock out of nothing more than petty spite.

He spits a litany of curses in Spanish.

"You ever wonder why he hates you so much?" Noah drains a tumbler and leaves the glass on the bar.

"I don't give a shit. And since when did you drink before noon?"

He wipes his mouth on the back of his sleeve. "Everyone has their vice."

I grab a bottle of the cheap shit from the bottom shelf and take a swig. The heat rushes down my throat and does its best to warm up the bone-deep chill I still feel from the creek. I replace the bottle and ignore my reflection in the bar mirror. Noah's drinking is something I need to address, but it will have to wait.

"You ready?" He glances at the stairs leading to the main level.

"As I'll ever be."

We climb the steps. The farther I rise, the heavier I feel. I want to ask my father about Delilah, but I can't. Uttering her name will put an even bigger target on her back. My father works in particular ways, ways that I've learned over years and years of watching him. Find out what people want themselves to be, then reflect that vision back at them. Even more important, find out what people fear, what they covet, what they care about, then twist it and use it to control them. He'd do the same thing with Delilah.

"Get in here!" My father's tone is jovial, so I naturally wonder what new bullshit he's cooked up to pile on us.

Miriam, former Maiden and current wife of the governor, sits on a couch to the right, her white skirt suit pitch perfect, and her tan legs crossed at the knee.

"The first lady came to see us." My father leans back in his chair, a smile stretching his too-tight lips.

"Miriam." I give her a nod as Noah and I sit in front of the desk.

"Nice to see you two." Her light blue eyes are sharp, missing nothing.

"Sweet Miriam was just telling me about a new

industry the governor is trying to woo into our great state. Tell me more." He waves at her to continue.

"It's a car manufacturer based in South Korea. They're looking to move to a state with a readily available workforce, room to grow, and of course, low taxes."

Dad scratches his chin. "Where are they looking to go in the state?"

"Somewhere along I-65 to the north of Birmingham. Likely Cullman County. They've got their eye on a hundred acres just off the highway and near the old Union Rail line. But they want some big tax breaks in exchange. Louis balked at that." She twirls a lock of hair around her finger and bites her lip in a practiced look of seduction. "He did at first, anyway."

My father pats his knee. Like an obedient dog, Miriam goes to my father and sits on his lap.

"You convinced him this would be a good deal, did you?" He nuzzles into her hair.

"I may have done a few things to change his mind." She unbuttons her jacket as my father's hands rove her body. "All for you, my Prophet."

"I want that company, especially if we can wrangle first pick on jobs for Heavenly members. Adam, go ahead and buy up the land Miriam is talking about. We'll want to sell it to the Koreans at a premium." He pulls her top down and sucks her nipple through her white lace bra.

Noah shifts in his seat and looks anywhere but at them.

"You think you can convince old Louis to set up a

meeting with us and the Koreans to talk work force?" He pulls her bra down and nuzzles her breasts.

"I can convince him."

"You can?" He grips her hair and pushes her down to the floor. "Show me how convincing you can be."

"Anything for you, Prophet." She licks her lips as she disappears behind the desk.

It's a relief that I can't see her anymore, even though sloppy wet sounds start up as my father leans back in his chair. My father is a pig, though no one seems to notice it but me.

"We'll get control of that car factory in no time." He grunts and tucks his hands behind his head. "A full Heavenly Ministries workforce running the place."

I don't look away from my father's filth. I never have. "I'll call the lawyer this morning."

"Get out of here, boys. I need to finish the rest of my business with Miriam." He closes his eyes as the slurping increases.

We walk out of the office and find Castro in the foyer staring daggers at me.

I laugh and stride past him, enjoying the extra fury that wrinkles his brow. He's a prick, and I've already decided I'll kill him one day. At this point, I'm just a cat playing with my food.

"Jeez." Noah exhales as we descend the stairs. "Dad just... he just does whatever."

"Prophet perks." I grab a top-shelf bottle from the bar. "And don't act surprised. He's done plenty worse than that."

He scrubs a hand down his face. "I mean, Mom is upstairs. Right now."

I unscrew the cap and take a drink of the dark, smoky liquor. Our mother may as well be on Mars. We can't get to her. Not with armed guards outside her door that track every move she makes, Castro her constant shadow when not guarding Dad. My father learned quickly after Noah and I made the biggest mistake of our lives. When he caught us trying to leave, he made us watch our mother pay for that mistake with interest. She's caged even more than we are.

"So you admit he's a disgusting pervert, but you still believe he talks to God and the devil?" I lean against the dark mahogany wood, my body sagging from too much effort and not enough fuel.

He shrugs. "He's still a man. Still flawed. But yes, I believe he's a prophet of the Lord. And that God and the Father of Fire are two sides of the same coin. He speaks to them."

I hold the bottle up to him in a half-ass salute. "Well, at least you're more fucked in the head than I am. I'll drink to that."

CHAPTER 5

DELILAH

*M*y old room. I sit on my bed, and it feels like a hundred years have passed since I was in this spot. I trace my fingers along the white bedspread.

A short knock at my door catches my attention, and Chastity walks in, both eyes black, a split lip, and bruising along her jaw. "Are you okay?" She hurries over to me.

"I'm fine." I keep tracing the bedspread as she examines my dress.

"No cross." She smooths the white fabric along my shoulders and lets out a breath of relief. "No cross."

"The Prophet didn't choose me." Tears well in my eyes, and shame washes over me like a tidal wave. "I offered myself to him, but he didn't take me." My lip trembles. "I'm not worthy of him. I know that now."

Chastity stiffens, then brushes the hair away from my face. "Delilah, what did they do to you? They kept me for two days and—" She unbuttons her shirt, then pulls it down to show red welts all over her fair skin. "Just beat-ings. On and on. But I've handled worse from them... Last time." She re-buttons her top and drops her voice to a whisper. "No one escaped. Not even Sarah. I think she's still in the Rectory." She swallows hard. "They saw the video where Susannah held the sharpened tooth-brush to my throat. I kept telling them I only climbed the fence to keep all of you in my sights so I could turn you in eventually."

I stare at her. She was right to try and turn us in. Being away from the Prophet is a horrible fate, one I never want to meet.

She continues on, her voice hushed, "They didn't believe me at first, but I stuck to it. Once the beatings stopped, they dragged me back here. But Grace trusts me even less now. Susannah, Eve, and Hannah are back in the Cloister. Subdued, but okay. What happened to you in the Rectory?"

"They showed me I was wrong. Foolish. Too stuck in this world when I should have been striving for the next." Tears flow down my face. "And the only way to get to paradise is to obey the Prophet."

She peers into my eyes, then runs her hands along my ribs. "You need to eat. They had you for four days and only fed you drugged fruit. Isn't that right?"

Indignation wells in me. "I wasn't drugged. The Prophet took care of me. He loves me."

"I'm going to see what I can find in the kitchen." She stands.

"I won't eat. Not until it's time. Not until the Prophet

says I can." I drop to my knees and turn toward the bed to begin my prayers. "I will spend all my time in praise of the Prophet. He's the only one who truly loves me." I cast a glance over my shoulder at her and can't help but smile. "I'm his favorite, you know?"

"Delilah, don't do this." She changes course and takes a spot next to me on the floor, her eyes growing wide. "Please don't."

"Don't do what?"

"Fall for it. You're too strong to believe the lies. Nothing the Prophet says is true. He's a deceiv—"

I launch myself at her and wrestle her to the floor. With a vicious slap, I yell in her face, "The Prophet is everything. Everything!" I hit her again with a smack so hard it vibrates up my arm and makes my teeth chatter.

She grips my wrists and throws me off, then rolls on top of me, pinning me against the cold wood floor. "Delilah." Her lip is split again, blood showing through the break in her skin.

"Get off me, witch!" I can't buck her. Whatever strength I had a moment ago is gone.

"Delilah, please." Her voice softens, but she keeps me in place. "Think about why you're here. Think—"

"For the Prophet."

"No." She shakes her head. "Not for him. You came here for *her*."

A ghost of a girl dances through my mind, her golden ringlets catching every ounce of sun. But it's as if I'm looking at her through a pane of frosted glass. She's there, though, waiting for me. The thought of her brings too much pain, so I push it away and focus on the Prophet. "No. I'm here for him. To serve *him*."

"When Georgia came here, she believed. But she had spirit." Her voice is low and even. "She managed to brighten the dark corners of the Cloister. No matter what happened to her, she kept going. She never broke, even after she stopped believing the Prophet's lies. She stayed strong. And she would have gotten away."

"You're lying!" I want to scratch her eyes out, to pull her tongue from her mouth. Who was she to cause me this pain? The pain that the Prophet had taken away.

"She told me about you."

"Lying whore!" I scream and try to fight her off. "Liar, liar, liar!"

She slams me back down.

The breath is knocked out of me, and I see stars, dark ones that flicker and burst. For a moment, there's a small sliver of clarity, as if I can see through the dark dream I'm in, but then it's gone. And I'm still here with Chastity, who insists on saying horrible things about the blessed Prophet. She's lying. She has to be. The Prophet is the only one who's ever told me the truth. Maybe ... maybe Chastity killed Georgia. Yes, that makes sense.

"You did it," I spit at her.

"What?" Her eyes widen. "I did what?"

"You killed Georgia. You're trying to throw your guilt onto the Prophet, because you are a filthy fallen creature. I know what sort of freak you are. The way you and Jez are too familiar. I know your sin. You're a disgusting Sodomite, and I hope the Prophet gives you what you deserve. Cuts your lying tongue out of your head! Murderer!"

Something like sadness creases the skin next to her eyes, but resolve still burns in her rough hold. She keeps her voice at a harsh whisper. "That's not true, and you know it. I would have never hurt Georgia. Think, Delilah! Remember why you came here. Fight it. Fight what he's done to you. Remember Georgia."

"Shut up." I wonder if I can throw her off and run, run to the Prophet and tell him about her lying ways.

"Do you remember her laugh?"

I blink. "What?"

"The way she would laugh. It was like light through leaves, warm and sweet."

A phantom sound plays through my mind, the warm, high notes of a carefree girl.

I clench my eyes shut when they begin to water. "No."

"And she would smile. Even when things were bad, even when training was horrible, even when Grace came down on her for being upbeat—she would smile, as if she knew everything would be all right. And I held onto that. I still do."

Georgia's smile breaks through the haze, and I remember her. I remember every aching detail. Her love, her light, her warmth. And I want it back—all of it—I want that lightness back so badly, but I'll never have it.

The Prophet's voice whispers to me, "Chastity killed her. Chastity took that light away. Chastity is the one who wants to hurt you. I am your salvation."

"You killed her."

"No." She shakes her head. "I loved her."

"Liar!"

"Georgia talked about her little sister with the white hair and the big heart, she—"

"Shut up." The tears burn and slip past my eyelids.

"She loved you so much and was glad you didn't follow her lead to this horrible—"

"You're lying." The frosted pane of glass that separates me from the laughing, golden-haired girl begins to crack.

"I'm not, Delilah. She told me what she used to call you to cheer you up."

"No." The cracks grow wider, fissures of light that show me a way out of this dark pit.

She leans down and presses her lips to my ears, speaking the name that only Georgia knew. That Georgia would call me when I was down or when things were even rockier with my mother than usual. Only Georgia. The frosted glass shatters.

My tears flow without stopping, and I choke out, "Georgia."

"She's lying." The Prophet's fingers brush along my heart. "I'm the true—"

"Shut up!" I snarl. "Liar! You're a liar. You—"

Chastity interrupts, thinking my words are meant for her. "I'm not lying. I was a brand new Spinner when I met Georgia—this was before I was sent to the Chapel. Before I tried to escape. We were friends. She was the only friend I ever had until I met Jez." Her eyes glisten, her tears matching my own. "She loved you so much. Do you remember? She told me all about you, and she was so glad that you were too smart to fall for the lure of this place. She loved you, and I loved her like a sister."

Her tears break through whatever tether is holding me, and I see Georgia fully in my mind. She's there, in all her youthful glory. Radiant, happy, and smiling at me. All the air leaves my lungs, as if someone punched me hard in the gut. She's gone. *Gone.* I can't fight the truth anymore, no matter how much it shreds me to bits.

The Prophet is the reason why I'll never get to hug my sister again. He laughs in my mind, but I don't feel his pull anymore, not when Georgia is shining brighter than a moonbeam in my memory.

Agony washes over me as I relive her loss, the funeral, the way she'd been tortured. I can barely push the words past my lips. "What happened to her?"

Chastity sits up and pulls me back to my knees until we're both 'praying' at the bedside. She doesn't look at the camera in the vent, but I know she's thinking about it. Just like I am.

I bow my head, letting the sting of loss hit me all over like a swarm of bees. My memory flickers—the Prophet staring down at me as I strip and spread my legs, offering myself to him. Bile rises in my throat, but I have no food to offer. I dry heave as Chastity remains still beside me.

"I very much want the gift you're offering, sweet Delilah." His gaze rests between my thighs. *"But you can serve me better as a pure angel of the Prophet."*

My stomach churns, but I clasp my hands together with a death grip and rest my sweaty forehead onto them.

Chastity leans closer. "It's the drugs. They build up in your system, especially if you take them every day. They form sort of a ... spider's web in your mind. You get trapped in it."

"You've been trapped?"

"I was when I was a Maiden. The weekly LSD is enough to start the threads. They grow stronger each time you eat the poisoned fruit. And then you're caught."

I wipe my eyes. "What happened to Georgia?"

"We don't know."

"We?"

She bites her lip, then winces. "We'll talk more later. I'm already going to be questioned about the video in here."

"Don't go."

She presses her shoulder into mine. "Stay strong." When she rises, I force myself to stay put even though I want to run after her and demand she tell me everything she knows about Georgia.

When she opens the door, I hear Grace's sharp voice. "I was just about to check in on you. You know you aren't supposed to be alone with the Maidens anymore."

"I know. My apologies. I just wanted to make sure she had everything she needed to resume training."

I don't turn around, just continue praying.

"She's fine. Go to the kitchen. You're on cook duty until I say otherwise."

"Yes, ma'am."

"And you." The Head Spinner's voice curls around my heart like barbed wire. "Just because the Prophet is giving you another chance doesn't mean I will. Step out of line one more time, and you'll find yourself back at the Rectory with no visits, no food, and no water except for that drip of water you love so much."

I jump as she slams my door shut, but even her threats can't stop the whirring in my brain. Chastity's information is just the kindling I need to keep going, to keep trying, and to finally get justice for Georgia. The Prophet broke me. I can't lie to myself and claim I stayed strong through the torture and the drugs. But Georgia has always been the thread that pulls me forward, the one touchstone that is always true. For once in my life, I actually bow my head in prayer and send a request so full of vengeance and retribution that I have no doubt heaven redirects it to a far hotter place.

I eat lunch with the others, though several of them assiduously avoid catching my gaze. Susannah, Eve, and Hannah all sit at separate tables, and I don't dare take a seat near any of them. I eat my small portion of vegetables and some sort of chewy meat alone. Every time the dining hall door opens, I look up in hopes of seeing Sarah. But it's never her.

Chastity works in the kitchen, but I only catch glimpses of her through the pass-through window. She keeps her head down, and I can't talk to her now, anyway.

A million questions burn inside me like dust from an exploding star. None of them will be answered, at least not today.

I'm relieved to find that, instead of training, we're doing TV time for the afternoon. I settle into my usual chair, though now it feels enormous. My body—once soft and with a few curves—is now waifish and weak. We all look like hell, but I suspect I appear worse than most. Physical and mental torture can do that to a person.

"Serve me, my precious one," the Prophet whispers. I clench my eyes shut and block out his voice. It's not real. Nothing he promised me is real. His whisper fades, and I can breathe again.

The door at the back of the room opens, and I wait for Abigail to tinker the projector on. Instead, Miriam Williams, the First Lady of Alabama, walks to the front of the room, her cream dress demure. She smiles, her perfect blonde hair and white teeth reminiscent of a skeletal doll—or am I imagining it?

"Good afternoon, Maidens." She snaps her fingers, and Abigail hurries over with a leather executive chair. Once she's settled, Miriam surveys the room. "I'm glad to see you all looking so well." Her gaze lingers on me for a moment before continuing on.

I look that bad?

She leans back. "You've been trained in the various ways of being a godly companion for your chosen mate. All the lessons you have learned up until this point are extremely important to your future. They may seem—" she taps her French-tipped nails on the arm of the chair

"—*difficult*, but they will pay off. They certainly have for me." Cue beauty queen smile. "Now, what I'm here to discuss in particular is the Christmas Eve celebration. The Prophet puts on a huge bonfire every year for Heavenly. You will all be in attendance, and you will be on your best behavior." She holds up a finger and crooks it. "Grace, would you care to explain?"

The Head Spinner walks to the front of the room. "Each one of you will be equipped with one of these." She holds up a necklace with a simple, but thick, chain with a cross hanging in the center. "I will assign a Spinner to watch each of you. Should you step out of line —Mary, get up here."

Mary rises from her seat in the back and walks to the front.

"Here." Grace hands her the necklace.

Mary takes it, but holds it away from her as if it's a venomous snake. Grace pulls a fob from her pocket.

Mary immediately shrieks and drops the necklace.

Grace smiles. "Apologies, Mary. I accidentally had it on the highest setting." She retrieves it and hands it to the shaking girl. "Hang onto it one more time for me."

This time when Grace uses the fob, Mary flinches, but doesn't make a sound.

"Thank you." Grace takes the necklace back and shoos Mary to her seat. "As you can see, these necklaces will punish any Maiden who steps out of line. I want you to keep in mind the Prophet's will when—"

"I can take it from here." Miriam's smooth voice holds a note of dismissal.

I take what little satisfaction I can in the fact that, in Miriam's presence, Grace is no longer the alpha. Grace gives her a sharp look, but nods and retreats as Miriam continues, "Now, after the initial bonfire ceremony where the Prophet will deliver his Christmas blessing, the Heavenly attendees will disperse. That is when your true test will begin."

I glance at Eve, but she seems rooted to her chair and stares at Miriam with an intensity that can only stem from hatred or fear. Which one, I can't tell.

"Suitors will be in attendance." She raises her eyebrows as if we're supposed to get excited. "Men who will express interest in those of you they find worthy. The Winter Solstice is a special time of year for the Prophet. You'll discover what I mean at the event. Now, I've instructed Grace on how I want all of you dressed and prepared. Looking our very best for the Prophet is a sure way to be in perfect obedience to him."

Her honey-coated words don't hide the truth. We're going to be exhibited like cattle at a meat market. I wrap my arms around myself more tightly.

She stands and paces back and forth gracefully, her stilettos barely making a sound on the wood floor. "There are certain rules that the Prophet will expect you to follow while at the celebration. You may not speak unless spoken to. You may not leave the common area. The suitors are special guests, but they are not to be trusted." She points to a Maiden on the front row. "You, come here."

The Maiden rises and walks over to her. I think her name is Phoebe.

Miriam pulls her dress up to her hips. Phoebe doesn't protest.

"The suitors will want to take this from you." She taps Phoebe between the legs. "This is your most sacred gift. If you dirty it with the touch of any man, you dirty your soul. The Prophet will know, and he will judge you."

My mind slingshots back to what Adam felt like inside me, filling every bit of me until all I could think of was him. My thighs clench. But I can't think about that. Not right now.

"You must keep this sacred, above all else. It is for the Prophet to take or give as he sees fit."

You mean it's the Prophet's to sell off. A suitor won't buy what's already been taken.

She drops Phoebe's dress back into place. "Protect your precious gift or face punishment. Do you understand?"

We nod.

She glares and shoves Phoebe toward her seat. "I said *do you understand?*"

"Yes," we yell in a torrent.

She composes herself and adopts her usual smile. "Good. I'm glad we're all on the same page. And now, I'll leave you to the rest of your training." She waves like a beauty contestant as she leaves the room, and we're all too shocked to whisper amongst ourselves as an ancient video about the importance of chastity begins to play.

CHAPTER 6

ADAM

*N*eed spurs me on faster and faster until I burst through the door to the dorms and rush to Delilah's room. When I fling her door open, she jumps and slides to the floor while yanking at her dress.

I want her in my arms so badly that I have to stop and take a breath. If I did that—simply embraced her—my father would see. And then my ruse would be over. She'd become an even bigger pawn in his game.

Forcing myself to take even steps is the worst torture I've ever endured, and I've been through plenty. I sit in front of her and simply stare at her. When I think about how she ran from me, I grip the edge of the bed. When I think about how I was willing to let her go, everything inside me rebels.

"Adam?" Her soft voice wafts over me, and something deep inside me begins to unwind.

I refocus on her gaze. Dark circles mar the skin under her eyes, her cheeks are gaunt, and her lips are cracked in several places. Raw wrists, slouching shoulders, and sallow skin tell me how bad it was in the Rectory. But they don't tell the whole story.

"What did they do, little lamb?" I stroke my hand down her cheek and find her just as warm as she's always been. "After you were led astray, what happened?"

"You took me to the Rectory." The bite in her voice cuts deep.

"I didn't have a choice." Did I? I could have let her go and killed the men closing in. But my mind plays through the outcomes. Each of them end with her captured and me dead or permanently entombed in the Rectory.

She drops her gaze, hiding her face from me. I'm supposed to tell her to look at me, to follow my rules, to always do what I say, and most of all—that any further disobedience will result in vicious punishment from me. Instead, I want to pull this wounded fairy with the broken wings into my arms. Fuck, I've gone soft.

"On the bed." Even though she's destroyed, my blood still thrills at the thought of touching her.

She doesn't resist, just climbs onto the mattress and lies on her back, even spreading her legs before I tell her to. I don't look at her there, despite the steady thrum of my blood telling me to. I lie down on top of her, balancing on my elbows and staring into her eyes. Gray and inscrutable, I wonder if I'll ever be able to look into them and see all of her.

"You can't try anything like that again." I keep my voice low, lest Grace and the Prophet got a little too exuberant and installed audio devices in Delilah's room. Hell, it's highly likely.

"I know."

I sift her hair between my fingers. "Tell me what happened in the Rectory." I need to know, to feel what she went through. If I could have taken the torture on myself, I would have. But my father didn't give me that option. He never gives me any options. I push the bitter truth aside and focus on my only respite from the Prophet. "I want to know."

"Aren't you going to threaten me first? Maybe hit me with your belt?" She comes out swinging, which I can appreciate.

"I only do that when it's fun." I glance down at her. "With you in this state, it would be like killing a fly with a bazooka. Flashy, but not satisfying."

"You're an asshole." The fire reappears in her, the flame that drew me from the moment I saw her.

"I know. Now tell me."

She closes her eyes, hiding from me. "I was strapped to a table. And there was water. Constant water." She touches a spot on her forehead and winces. "It dripped. And I know it sounds insane, but that drip... it was so—"

"It's a form of torture as old as civilization." I press my forehead to hers, trying to erase the ghost of sensation she's feeling.

"Good to know." She clears her throat. "And it was pitch black. Grace was there. She'd taunt me."

Murderous rage boils inside me, but I stay relaxed, as calm as I can be to soothe her nightmare away. "Yes."

47

"And they would drag me to this room. And..."

I wait for her to continue and catch a tear rolling from the corner of her eye. The words "you're safe now, with me" hover on the tip of my tongue, but they aren't real. They're lies. And I can't force them past my lips. A first.

"Your father would be there. With food and water." The words pour out of her in an anguished torrent. "And I couldn't say no. I was so hungry and tired and, God, I just wanted it to stop and he kept telling me all these things." More tears leak from the corners of her eyes, and I wipe each one away. "He was so kind, but then I would be dragged back to that room. Again and again."

"I'm sorry." The apology is rusty coming from me. But I mean it all the same.

"Sorry?" She gives me an incredulous stare. "You sent me there! You could have let me go. You could have let all of us go. You can end this right now!"

"Keep your voice down." I grip her forearms. "And I can't end this, not now. There are so many things you don't know—"

"I'm well aware that I'm in the dark."

"And you're going to have to stay that way, I'm afraid." I can't tell her my plans, the things I want for her —for us.

"Get out." She tries to pull her arms free, but can't. "Please just leave."

She's closed off again, nothing getting through her armor. I lean close to her ear. "Check under your pillow, little lamb. But don't let them see." I rise and stride to the door, leaving her room without looking back. Each step away from her is a new scar across my soul, but she needs to recover. And I only have two days to finish preparations for the Winter Solstice.

The Spinners drop their chins in deference as I tear through the hallways until I come to Grace's door. It swings open. She's been watching me from the moment I set foot in The Cloister. Bitch.

"To what do I owe this little visit?" She perches on the edge of her desk as I sink into one of her too-plush leather chairs.

"Are you going to hold up your end for the Solstice?"

"Of course." She runs her fingers along a silver necklace sitting on the edge of her desk. "My Maidens will fall in line. I've been in constant communication with the Chapel. They're ready. What about you?" Her eyes narrow. "Do you have your end straight?"

I nod. "Bonfire, entertainment, sacrifice."

Her eyes dance at that last word. I want to pity the creature she's become, but I can't bring myself to pardon her for any of her sins. She's a jagged piece of filth, just like me. And to forgive her would be hollow, empty like we are. What she's done is beyond *grace*. I would laugh at the irony, but nothing can make me smile. Nothing except Delilah.

"Have you changed your mind about what I said last time?" She begins to lift her skirt.

"Knock it off." I hold her gaze.

Her perfect pout forms as she drops the fabric. "Still mad?"

"Stop terrorizing Delilah." I take an ounce of joy when she winces.

"She's my Maiden. The Prophet has given me leave to do what—"

"If I find another bruise, break, or so much as a scratch on her, I'll be back here for you."

"Is that supposed to be a threat?" She bats her lashes.

"Do you know the spot on the river about half an acre from where Faith is buried?" Just saying her name opens a wound that never truly stopped bleeding. But this needs to be done, and I have to do it now.

She blanches and walks around her desk, foolishly believing that a chunk of mahogany can protect her from me. "Why are you saying this?"

"Because that's the spot where I will drown you. I've thought about that deep water so many times." I stare at her, seeing every bit of her twisted heart and broken soul. "The rocks there are smooth, did you know? The water has cleared off their rough edges over time. So, when I step into that dark pool, I'll do it barefoot, feeling those round rocks beneath my toes. You'll be thrashing, scream-ing, begging. Your dress will soak with water. It's so cold there under the oak trees, even in the summer, the water will give you a chill." She crosses her arms as I stand and walk over to her, continuing, "You'll keep running your lying mouth, just like you always do, and I'll shove you under the surface. And then?" I lean down and grab her chin, squeezing it hard. "Blissful silence. I'll leave your body there. No one will find you. I'll forget about you, and before long you'll be food for fish, raccoons, coyotes.

And then you'll just be gone." I smile down at her, her eyes wide and her mouth slack.

"Adam," she whispers, her eyes watering.

Her tears don't affect me, not anymore. I hope she sheds enough to drown herself.

"Don't. Touch. Delilah." Releasing her, I turn and stride out the door.

CHAPTER 7

DELILAH

*S*unday church service starts with a choir of children on the stage in front of me. Boys and girls in all white with glittery haloes made from silver garlands hovering above their crowns. Most of them are barely past toddler age, none of them over five, and they sing about Christmas in a disjointed, cute fashion.

I smile at them from beneath my veil, even though I'm tired. The food Adam slipped me the night before had gone a long way toward putting me to rights, but I'm still worn thin. I look forward to afternoon prayers in my room, where I can nap instead of telling God how great the Prophet is.

Adam catches my eye as he helps some of the children offstage at the end of their number. He treats them with a warmth I didn't think possible, smiling pleasantly and patting some of them on the back as they toddle away. He's good with children—the thought strikes me like an odd flash, heat lightning on a summer afternoon.

Once the children are settled in the rows behind us, the Prophet walks onto the stage and delivers his Christmas sermon once the applause dies down.

"We are here to give thanks to our Lord and Savior, to praise Him and celebrate the day of His birth."

"Amen" rockets around the sanctuary.

"We are also here to plan for our bright future, just as Mary and Joseph did for their little baby in swaddling clothes. Though they had nothing but a child and gifts from the wise men, they were able to raise the son of God. We have so much more." He raises his hands. "We have each other. We have the strength of our beliefs. And we have the conviction to see God's plan through to the end."

Adam keeps his gaze on mine. I can feel it even when I have to drop my eyes lest anyone notice I'm not the demure Maiden I'm supposed to be.

"Many of you have already applied for housing in Monroeville. The houses are going up even faster than I anticipated, and the Lord is pleased. In addition to the housing, we're clearing land, tilling fields, creating farm-land, and purifying water from the Lockahatchee River that runs through the compound." His voice rises, crowned by notes of triumph. "By the end of next year, Heavenly will be completely self-sufficient."

The crowd erupts, each lost soul clamoring for the love and safety promised by the charlatan on stage.

"Each of you will make this possible. And God smiles on you for doing it. Here, we will be safe from the coming wars, from the sodomites and the multitude of demons that run this fallen world. We will arm ourselves to defend against those who would seek to destroy us. They are Legion, my friends. Sinners, adulterers, murderers, rapists, liberals, feminists, politicians, Catholics, Jews, Muslims—any and all who deny the divinity of Christ, who would deny the teachings of the Bible—apostates! And they *will not stop* until all of God's blessed creation is a smoking ruin." The fervor from his voice spills into the worshippers behind me, ramping up the wild energy to dangerous heights. "But we will beat them. With God on our side, we are guaranteed to triumph over evil. Together, we will create a new Eden, where we will work to please God and no one else. We will have no other masters. We are chosen. We are God's most precious children. You—" He points to the crowd "—are the jewels in the crown atop Jesus' head."

The floor shakes beneath me as the Heavenly audience jumps to their feet and gives the Prophet a standing ovation. Adam scowls, his arms folded in front of him. Noah stands just behind him, his gaze fixed on the Prophet as he applauds along with everyone else. I didn't realize it, but Noah is a true believer. I'd assumed he was like Adam, jaded and wise. I was wrong.

When the fervor settles down, the Prophet continues, "But there must be sacrifice, my friends. We must all give something to the Lord. We must all be more godly." His voice softens, curtailing the fever pitch and pulling the audience in closer. "Tithing is important. And I can easily say I'm proud of how our Heavenly family gives to keep this ministry going. But we must give more. Monetarily, and in other avenues. How many of you have your children in the fallen public schools or worse, the supposedly 'Christian' schools that are nothing more than breeding grounds for sin?"

The crowd remains utterly silent.

"I'm here to tell you right now that Heavenly schools are the path for your children's salvation. You must enroll them now, before it's too late."

Agreement rumbles behind me.

"And women, your men are sacrificing their head of the household income, but what are you giving? Are you in perfect obedience? Perhaps you think you are, but look down right now. All of you, look down. Can you see your bare legs? If you can, I'm here to tell you that you are *not* in perfect obedience. Are you wearing pants that leave nothing to the imagination? If you are, I'm here to tell you that you are *not* in perfect obedience. Are you showing your body to men other than your husband? If you are—" he shakes his head and tsks "—I can assure you that you are not in perfect obedience. Women are sacred treasures and should be treated as such. But how can men treat you as godly when you dress like common prostitutes? When you do everything you can to inflame their lust?" He drops to one knee, as if he's proposing to all the women in the audience. "I humbly ask you now, as your Prophet, to sacrifice your *vanity*. To be pure and holy for your husbands. And even if you aren't wed, to dress as a woman of worth, not of a worldly harlot. These are the small sacrifices the Lord requires of you." He casts his gaze heavenward. "Do you think you can do these things, for Him?"

Shouts of "yes" rise to another crescendo.

I squeeze my hands so tightly I fear I've drawn blood. But I don't move.

The Prophet points into the crowd. "Sister, where are you going?"

I cast a look behind me. A woman stands on a side aisle, a little girl pulled close against her as Protectors and a handful of Heavenly officers close in around her. She's far away, but I can sense her protective stance, see her backing away.

"Why do you run from the Lord's truth?" The Prophet shakes his head and rises to his feet.

The Heavenly officers take her by the elbows, and a Spinner grabs her daughter. They are marched out of the sanctuary, and I can only imagine what will happen to them.

"Fallen women are, sadly, rampant in this world." He turns back to his flock, a benevolent smile on his face, the fatherly nature of his words smoothing over the scene's discomfort. "But we can save them. And we will, with God's blessing."

Applause. The audience actually applauds what just happened, and I feel sick. The Prophet's words disgust me, but no one else seems to feel the hatred and misogyny seeping from him. No one except Adam. His scowl has deepened, and now he's glaring at his father. He's forgotten himself, let his mask of obedience slip. Relief is too vague a word for what washes over me when I see the naked hatred in Adam's eyes.

Once the Prophet is satisfied that the crowd is onboard, he turns toward discussing the night of Christ's birth, and the star that led the wise men to Him. It's an empty homily after his calls for hatred of anyone outside of these walls. But Adam seems to relax as the Prophet treads less fervent ground.

I shoot a glance to my right. Sarah's spot is empty. Her loss is a nagging rot in my gut. Why would they keep her at the Rectory for so long? I have to assume she received the same torture as I did. A shudder rushes through me as I feel the ghost tap from the ever-dripping water. I clasp my hands together so hard that my knuckles turn white and pull myself together. Sarah, I need to focus on her. Maybe Chastity can find out what's going on?

Once the Christmas sermon ends, the Maidens rise and file out of one of the side doors. The children from the rows behind us mill around in the wide hallway, playing chase or speaking to each other in words only toddlers can understand. The Prophet sweeps down from backstage and grabs the first child he comes across, swinging the boy up and hugging him.

"And how are you today, Elias?"

The boy, no more than three, squirms and grins as the Prophet tickles him.

Adam stands at the top of the stage stairs, a silent hawk.

I can't help but stare at the curious scene unfolding

before me. The Prophet seems to genuinely care about the children. He sets Elias down, then kneels to speak to a little blonde girl, her dark eyes wide as he pulls a piece of candy from his pocket and hands it to her.

"What do you say?" a Spinner behind the girl prompts.

"Thank you." She clutches the candy to her chest as the Prophet kisses her on the forehead. There's a familiarity to it that stops me, and I look up at Adam. His stone countenance gives nothing away, but he's watching me just as closely as he watches his father.

I peer down the long hallway where churchgoers are exiting the sanctuary. No adults walk toward the children, no parents coming to claim their little ones. Only the Prophet, greeting each child by name. My mouth goes dry as the suspicion blooms into more, and I remember Adam telling me that there's a worse fate than being sent to the Chapel.

"Go." A Maiden pushes me forward as the Spinners herd us away from the Prophet and my grim theories.

CHAPTER 8

ADAM

The constant thump of hammers fills the morning air. The piles of pallets and firewood stand ready at the center of the clearing, and construction is almost finished on the pavilions on each side of the pyre.

Tony strides over, a steaming thermos in his hand. "Want some?"

"No thanks." I keep my arms crossed and watch the finishing touches go up—crosses on the front of each pavilion, chairs and benches arranged in neat rows on the wooden floors, plenty of room for the Heavenly multitude. For a moment, I wonder if I can douse the whole place with gas so that they go up right along with the bonfire. Then again, despite their misplaced faith, most of the churchgoers don't deserve that fate. I turn my gaze toward the most ornate of all the structures. Now, there's a good spot to dump lighter fluid. The Prophet and all his top minions will be gathered there. I scowl. Delilah will be there, too. And Noah. And, if my father is feeling particularly cruel, my mother. It would seem like the perfect opportunity to strike, but my father will be surrounded by Protectors and goons. He won't leave my mother unattended. If I go anywhere near her, things will get dicey.

"Sir?" Tony furrows his brow. He's been talking, apparently.

"What?"

"I was just saying that everything is fixing to be ready. And I can make sure it's all done. If you, you know, have more important things to do, then I can—"

"Trying to get rid of me, Tony?"

He takes a step back. "No-no, sir. I was just—"

"Calm down. I was kidding."

He doesn't calm. I find it gratifying that plenty of the Heavenly faithful seem to fear me far more than my father. "I'll head out. Call me if there's any trouble."

"Will do." He tries on a strained smile.

I turn and head back to my car, then drive the narrow lane toward the main buildings. I know the road by heart, could drive it blindfolded by this point. My thoughts return to Delilah. I won't get to see her alone tonight. The Spinners will prepare each Maiden for the bonfire. They must look good for all the prospective buyers, after all. My grip tightens on the wheel as I think of Delilah being dangled in front of the predators coming to sample the Prophet's wares.

The vain hope that I can keep her away from them can't even flicker to life in my chest. She's a part of my father's game. Just like I am. We're damned, all of us. The thought stings me like a thousand hornets burrowing into my skull.

I ease to a stop and finally pay attention to the landscape. No longer on the main road, I've turned off and driven to the one sunny spot on this entire cursed compound. A small rise, one you'd miss for the trees growing up around it.

I didn't intend to come here.

Putting the car into park, I get out and walk through the undergrowth, my shoes scuffing the bed of pine needles as I climb. When I exit the woods, the sun warms the top of my head and the tall grass, gray with winter, brushes against my legs.

A small mound is the only sign that an angel lies buried beneath the Alabama dirt. I sink to my knees next to my Faith and close my eyes. Her sweet smile flashes through my mind—chubby cheeks, dark eyes, a patch of strawberry blonde hair on her head.

"Remember when you walked to me?" I can see her, unsure feet and a look of determination on her face. She wobbles back and forth, then takes a step and falls into my arms. Grace cheers and leans down to give Faith a kiss on her fuzzy crown.

The memory disintegrates. It fades, washing away, becoming nothing—just like my perfect Faith.

"She's sick. She needs a doctor." I cradle Faith close to my chest as she struggles to draw breath.

"You break my commandment and sully a Maiden,

then want me to go against God's will and let you take the bastard child to a doctor?" My father scowls.

"She's sick!" I lower my voice when Faith starts to cry. "I have to get her to a doctor."

"If she's sick, it's God's will."

"Grace." I turn to her, our child in my arms. "We can't keep her here. She'll die."

She looks at me, eyes wide, then back at my father. "I—"

"Grace, listen to me. If you take that child from the compound, your soul will rot in eternal torment for going against the will of God. Heavenly's gates will be closed to you. You've already sinned against me by fornicating with Adam. Don't make it worse."

"Grace." I try to wrench her attention away from him, but she wouldn't look at me. At us.

"This is God's will." My father slams his hand onto his desk. "And you will not circumvent it!"

"Grace, please."

"The Prophet is right." She finally turns toward me, her eyes hard despite the tears running from them. "If Faith dies, then it's His will."

I take a few steps backwards. "I'm taking her. She's not going to die here because of your crazy bullshit."

My father waves a hand.

Something cracks against the back of my skull. I can't see. Then I'm falling. Faith. Where is my Faith?

"I want to hold you." A blast of chilly air whips through the woods, the trees groaning and swaying. "Like I did when you were first born, like I did when we would play peekaboo, or when I'd rock you to sleep. I held you when you were sick, too. I held you all the time, remember? I couldn't bear to put you down. Not even at the end, when you closed your eyes and snuggled against me. Your sweet breaths growing slower and slower. You stopped struggling. Because your tiny body was so tired, sweet girl. And I knew I had to let you go." I clench my eyes shut and remember the locked door, the room in the basement of my father's house, my wails of agony that went unanswered.

I let the pain hit me again, the loss, the anger. "That was my father's one kindness, letting me hold you as you drifted away, back to whatever sweet heaven you came from. I didn't deserve you. And I failed you." I press my hand to the grassy mound as the sun hides behind a cloud. "I'm sorry."

I don't cry. Not because I'm tough. When it comes to Faith, I'm not. But I save up all my pain, my loss, my anger, and I direct it into something so much darker. My vengeance is like a storm that forms slowly, the hot earth sending energy into the air as I boil and bubble and grow into a black anvil that will rain hell down on my enemies. My time is coming. "*Our* time, sweet angel. It's almost here."

Leaning down, I kiss the ground that's covered my sleeping Faith for the past four years. I don't have to tell her I love her. She'll know when the Prophet's blood covers my hands.

CHAPTER 9

DELILAH

The door to my room bursts open, and the Spinner who's been working on my makeup jumps and almost pokes me in the eye with a mascara wand.

"Out!" Adam's bellow spurs the Spinner into action. She scurries out the door, and he slams it behind her.

"What are you—"

He bowls me over, pressing his mouth to mine with an insistence that scares me. His tongue lashes mine as he scoots me up on the bed, his elbow sending the Spinner's makeup palette crashing to the floor.

I can smell the outside on him, feel the chill in the fibers of his clothes as they press against my naked body. He settles between my thighs and focuses on the complete domination of my mouth. My shock turns to something more liquid as he destroys me with each wicked stroke of his tongue.

He pulls away and bites my neck, and I gasp in air.

Slipping a hand beneath me, he squeezes my ass hard enough to hurt, and pulls me against his thick erection. A shudder courses through me at the rough contact, and I tangle my fingers in his hair.

Working his way to my breasts, he nips at me, then takes my nipple into his mouth, sucking the stiff peak until I'm writhing beneath him. But he doesn't stop grinding me against his cock, my body open and wanting despite everything. Adam has this power over me, and I'm not sure I mind anymore. I pull his hair, and he groans, switching to my other nipple and biting down.

I should stop him, ask him what's going on, tell him to fuck off for turning me in to the Rectory. But none of that rises past my lips. Instead, "I need you," falls out on a heavy breath.

"Fuck." He kisses down my stomach, his warm breaths sending goosebumps racing across my skin.

He doesn't wait, doesn't tease, just dives in, his tongue stroking my entrance, then moving up to my clit. I jerk, but his hands come down on my hips, holding me in place as he feasts on me. I struggle and surge, chasing every ounce of pleasure he offers. He backs off for a moment, and I bite my lip. When he slaps my pussy, I jerk and pull his hair, but he's already fastened his mouth to the burn caused by his rough palm, his tongue soothing the ache and infusing it with desire.

Another slap has me crying out, then he hits me again and again, my swollen clit throbbing with each pop from his fingers.

I look down and catch his gaze. The lust in his eyes

almost shatters me, and when he hits me again, I feel my orgasm racing toward me, seizing every muscle and demanding every bit of energy. I gasp, and he presses his lips to my clit, sucking and biting down. Then he presses two fingers inside me, massaging the place he's already marked as his.

I come on a silent scream, my breath caught in my throat, my thighs wide, my body frozen and then melting in a surge of heat. Wave after wave crashes down on me, drowning me in a bliss that I've only ever felt with Adam. He doesn't stop licking, his fingers pumping as my walls clamp down around him. His groan vibrates through me, and I arch my back, wringing every last bit of pleasure from his mouth. When the waves lessen, I relax into the bed, my body sated and my mind adrift.

With a rough yank, he pulls me onto my stomach. I can't protest. I'm boneless, weightless. His palms spread my cheeks, and when his tongue presses against my asshole, awareness races back to me.

"Adam—" I can barely get the word out. He slips his fingers into me again, massaging me with my own wetness. Then he pulls it to my ass, rubbing around my hole, then pressing one finger inside.

I moan, and he yanks my hips up. He keeps rubbing my slick hole, then squeezes his finger deeper. This is nothing like the violation of the butt plugs. His touch sends heat racing through me and pooling in my stomach. My aching muscles begin to tense again, everything drawing tighter and tighter. When I hear his zipper, I turn and look at him. He's shirtless, every muscle in his body drawn taut.

His eyes are shadowy pools of need. "I hope you're ready, little lamb."

I swallow hard. "I don't know."

"I do." He pushes his cock head against me, and I lean forward. Grabbing a handful of my hair, he pulls me back. "Don't move."

The pressure grows, and I bite my lip as his head slips inside.

"Ah fuck." He pushes harder, and I yelp from the pain.

"You have to take it, little lamb. I want you to feel all of me." He leans over me and presses his forehead to my back. "I own every fucking piece of you, little lamb. Your ass is mine." He pushes farther in, and I clutch the bedspread.

He reaches around, his fingers brushing my stomach, and starts stroking my clit. I curl my toes as he draws my focus to the swipes and dips of his fingertips. When he's pushed fully inside me, pain wars with arousal.

"So tight. Fuck." He bites my back, an animal keeping its mate in place. My body quivers under his possession, each of us slick with sweat.

His fingers don't stop their dizzying tease of my clit, and he doesn't let up as he pulls out and sits back on his knees. He spits, and I look back at him, his gaze on my ass as he pushes inside again. "Look at you." He groans. "Just fucking look at you, taking every inch in your sweet virgin ass."

I let my head drop onto my pillow, my ass in the air as he starts a slow fuck, each plunge inside verging on pain but hovering on pleasure. He slips his fingers inside me again. "Goddamn." Pulsing forward, he fills every bit of me with him. His cock, his fingers, his voice in my ear, his dark heart beating with mine.

I push back against him, and he grabs my ass. "That's it." With a slap that resounds through the room, he pushes inside me faster. I want the punishment, need to feel him deep. He grips my shoulder and pulls me up to him, his chest to my back.

He tugs my hair until I crane my neck around and he kisses me hard while thrusting inside me. Everything is rough—our kiss, his fucking, and his hands roving my body. He slaps my breast, then grips it hard. I moan into his mouth, my legs still wide as he brings his fingers back to my clit. Tiny explosions burst through my body as he pinches my nipple and strokes me, his cock embedded deep inside me, and touching secret places with each hard thrust.

We are joined, my hands up behind his neck, our bodies moving and grinding as arousal blots out everything except our animal need for each other.

His fingers move faster, pushing me to the brink. I open my mouth as my body seizes again. I moan low and long into his mouth as my orgasm crashes down like a deluge. He shoves me down onto the bed, and with a hard grunt, pulls out. I'm lost in my pleasure as hot jets of come lash across my ass, and his groan rattles to the very core of my soul.

My legs give out, and I ease down to the bed, lying flat on my stomach and trying to catch my breath. He lands on his side next to me, his breath ragged as he brushes the hair away from my face, the strands wet with sweat.

I can't speak, only meet his gaze. Something passes between us. A silent communion of our souls. I can't say it's forgiveness, because I'm not ready for that yet, not so soon after the Rectory. But it's the acknowledgement of our bond—the one that began the night of the bonfire, and the one that was cast in iron the night he took my virginity.

He strokes my cheek softly with his thumb. The fire is momentarily doused. I smile at his gentle touch. His eyes widen a little. Is he surprised?

"I know I hurt you." His voice is like shards of stone, and I don't know if he's talking about turning me in to the Rectory or what just happened between us.

Either way, the answer is the same. "Yes."

He strokes a hand down my back. "I like hurting you, little lamb."

I should be repulsed. Instead, a flicker of heat fires inside me. "I know."

"I have to go." He pulls back and, for the first time since he barreled into my room, casts a glance at the camera.

"I'm pretty sure the Spinner is going to lose her shit when she sees—" I gesture toward my face before dropping my too-tired arm back to the bed.

He rises and zips up his pants, then snatches his shirt from the floor. "You don't need any of that shit."

I smile, my lips swollen from his rough kisses. "Did you just compliment me?"

He smirks and runs a hand through his hair. "Yes, and I'll do it a second time. I'm going to take that perfect, tight ass again the first chance I get. So be ready." He walks into the bathroom, then returns with a warm washcloth. "I hate to do this." He swipes at my ass, cleaning me, his voice barely a whisper. "You should always have some of me in you, on you, fucking everywhere." He bites my shoulder, then rises. "Clean the rest of it up yourself," he says loud enough for any listening device to hear and tosses the wadded washcloth on the floor with a smirk.

Whatever storm raged inside him is quiet now. His easy confidence is back, the usual darkness, the quiet air of control. *I did that.* Am I the music that can calm the beast?

Without a goodbye, he strides from the room. A few gruff words in the hall sends my Spinner rushing back inside. I sit up, and her gaze travels over the love bites on my neck and my breasts. She tsks and kneels, collecting the bits of the makeup kit.

I stare at the door long after he's gone, wondering about the tempest that blew him to my bed.

Will I ever know what makes him tick?

CHAPTER 10

ADAM

*C*hristmas music wafts through the foyer of the Prophet's home, and dignitaries mill about. The Christmas Eve bonfire draws the filth of the earth like moths. Senators, governors, CEOs—they're all here drinking and carousing in the hour before the ceremony is set to start.

"And this is my son, Adam." My father pulls me into a conversation he's having. "Adam, this is Senator Roberts."

I force a smile and shake hands with the man. He's mid-thirties and trim. I'm certain I've seen him before.

"Nice to meet you. Your father is truly a man of God. And I've learned some new, Biblical teachings during my visits to the Chapel here at Heavenly." He grins broadly at his too on-the-nose joke.

"We're glad to have you." I keep the fake smile, and it works, because the senator takes another drink from his glass.

"The Senator is here looking for the future Mrs. Roberts."

"We have plenty of Maidens that I'm certain will spark your interest." I take a crystal glass from a passing tray. Champagne, of course.

"I think I already have my eye on a certain one."

"Oh? How so?" I don't miss my father's grin.

"I ran into one at the Chapel. She didn't belong there. But she certainly whet my whistle for more of what she had to offer."

I grip my glass too hard. The only Maiden I know of that's been to the Chapel is Delilah.

"Well, you'll have the pick of the litter, I can assure you." My father claps him on the back and shoots me a pointed look. "I need to go over final preparations with Adam for this evening, but please make yourself at home. If there's anything you need, you simply have to ask."

"Will do." Roberts raises his glass to my father, then turns to mingle in the crowd—most of them potential suitors for one of my father's Maidens.

I follow my father to his office. He closes the double doors and walks around his desk.

Castro isn't here. As that knowledge sinks in, my blood begins to pound, beating a violent rhythm in my ears. Has the Prophet just unknowingly given me a gift? I move toward the chairs as my father flicks on the screen behind him. Delilah and I are there, our bodies moving as I fuck her.

"I really enjoyed this show." He turns toward the screen.

I edge closer. There's a heavy paperweight in the shape of a cross I can use to do it. Expedient. Though I'd rather use my bare hands.

"Did you know your Maiden's cunt looks like a lily, the lightest shade of pink on earth? She showed me, opened her legs wide and offered me everything." Satisfaction punctuates every one of his words.

They sting, but not as much as they could. I've already tasted the heaven between her thighs, and she's given me everything. My father will never be able to touch what Delilah and I shared.

I'm at the side of the desk, moving slowly as my father stares at the video. He's just the sort of degenerate who can get his rocks off while watching his son fuck someone.

A few more steps and I'll be close enough to strike. My fingers graze the paperweight. I slow my breathing, a calm falling over me. It always feels like this when I'm about to deliver the death blow. Serene. The calm before the burst of adrenaline and the splash of blood.

"She's rare. The way she looks like a ghost, that weird hair and eyes. Senator Roberts took a shine to her right off. He's already made an offer."

One more step. I take it, the paperweight in my palm.

My hands go cold, lethal. I can see the pulse in his leathery neck. This is it.

"I won't accept it, of course. It's not good enough. And she needs more time at The Cloister." He shrugs, completely unaware of the viper at his back.

I raise my hand. I'll bludgeon him, wrestle him to the

floor, then squeeze the life out of him. Hide his body, rush upstairs, grab Mom, then over to Noah's place, then to the Cloister. I'll kill whoever I have to if it means our freedom.

It's all right there, within my grasp.

The door opens.

Castro steps in and reaches for the piece in his chest holster.

My heart thumps out of rhythm, and I replace the paperweight, then step back and lean against the desk.

Castro narrows his eyes. "What were you doing?" His hand is on the butt of his pistol.

"Watching a little bit of action, thanks to—" My father turns, and his eyes widen when he finds me right next to him. He blanches, then stumbles backwards.

"What?" I smirk, enjoying the fear that paints his face. He needs to be scared more often, needs to realize that no one's life is eternal, not even his.

"You have the look of death about you. You were going to—"

"Kill you with a house full of politicians and law enforcement?" *Yes I was.* "Not a chance."

"Step away, asshole." Castro pulls his gun.

I hold my hands up and walk around the desk, then sink into a chair. "Why so jumpy?"

My father swallows hard, then swipes a hand across his face. "Nest of rattlesnakes." He scowls at me.

In the video, I pull Delilah upright so she's sitting on my cock as I pound inside her. "Can I get a copy of this?"

Castro holsters his pistol and stares. I don't even want

to think about him popping wood while watching Delilah. My blood demands vengeance. I lean my head back on the chair, the picture of ease while my thoughts race. I was so close, so fucking close. Did I hesitate?

"Never alone, Castro. Not with him." My father points at me. "You know better."

"Sorry." Castro bows his head. "I had to take a piss."

"Take a piss on your own fucking time!" My father's voice shakes, likely cutting through the "Oh Come, All Ye Faithful" playing in the rest of the house.

"You're afraid?" I cock my head to the side as if I'm surprised. "Why on earth would you be afraid of your own son?"

"Don't play games with me, boy." He slams the controller, pausing the recording right when I shoot my load all over Delilah's perfect ass. I really do want the video.

"No games. Was there something you wanted besides this?" I point to the screen.

My father sits and yanks open his drawer. It's powder time.

"I wanted to double-check the preparations. The Father of Fire is expecting an extravagant tribute."

"Everything's in order." I've triple-checked everything with Grace. If a single bow of fucking holly is out of place, I'll be shocked as hell.

"It better be." He snorts a line, then pinches the powder off his nostrils. "If anything goes wrong, I'm inclined to sacrifice you to the Father of Fire in payment."

"Do what you have to do." I inspect my nails. "But everything is set. The Maidens will look like whores. The whores will look like whores. Alcohol and drugs once the congregants leave. And everyone will have a good time."

He sits back, his beady eyes focused on me. "Don't disappoint me."

"I hate to break my disappointment streak, but tonight, you'll be happy with me."

He waves an annoyed hand at me. I'm dismissed.

I rise and walk to the doors. When I touch the handles, he says, "Don't think I don't know what's in your heart, Adam." He uses the gentle voice, the one steeped in a coercion so soft it feels like silk. "The Lord has warned me about you. He's also promised me that I won't die by your hand. So whatever plans you have, you may as well abandon them, son. They won't come to fruition."

"Good to know." I open the door and stalk out, slamming it behind me.

A few heads turn, but most of them go back to their drinks and their chatter. I don't have time for niceties.

Grace beelines toward me, her ridiculous black habit blowing behind her. I turn and head down the stairs. She follows.

"What?" I stop at the bar and pour myself a stiff one, not offering her a single drop.

"I just wanted to tell you all the girls are ready." She casts a glance toward the far side of the basement, towards the door with the bar leaning against the wall next to it.

I slam the booze back and pour another.

"Did you hear me?" She steps closer.

"Yes." I bite the word off and swallow the second drink.

"Adam." She reaches out, her fingers brushing my arm. I toss my glass down and turn to leave.

She won't leave me alone, not till she says whatever the hell she came here to say. I know her too fucking well.

I stop. "Spit it out. I have shit to do."

She fidgets with the edge of her habit. "Aren't you even going to ask why I did it?"

"Why you did what?"

She moves even closer. "Lied for you," she whispers. "The day you fucked that slut."

I can't kill her here, no matter how much I want to. It wouldn't be difficult to drag her to the room where she let Faith die in my arms, but I refuse to tarnish that space with Grace's blood. "I can only assume it's because you want something out of it." I meet her gaze, hatred sizzling beneath my skin.

Her lip trembles. "I'm sorry."

"You don't get to say those words to me, Grace." I keep my hands off her, though the thought of cracking her neck still brings untold comfort.

"I was young and stupid and still under his influence." The words pour out, and I can hear the truth in them, but it doesn't change my mind.

"You can't make up for Faith, Grace. You can lie for me, help me, follow my every command, but I will *never* forgive you. Next time you have me over a barrel, I suggest you drown me. Because if you don't, I'll come for you one day." I turn on my heel as tears streak down her face.

"Adam—" her voice breaks as she sinks to the floor.

She's broken, but I can't fix her.

Fuck, I can't even fix myself.

CHAPTER 11

DELILAH

"*B*est behavior." Grace walks down the line of Maidens, baton in her hand. "What does that mean to you?" She stops just ahead of me and tilts Eve's chin up with her baton. "Answer, Maiden."

"Only speak when spoken to." Her small voice trembles. "Don't embarrass the Prophet. And, um—"

"And," Grace broaches.

"Protect my Maidenhood."

"Correct." Grace continues past me, her eyes red-rimmed. I could swear she's been crying, but that doesn't quite square with what I know about the Head Spinner. My fingers flex instinctively, the small one on my right hand aching where she broke it. Abigail hasn't bothered to replace the splint since my time in the Rectory, but says it should heal straight on its own.

"Tonight, you must shine for the Prophet. I don't feel that I need to explain what will happen to you if you don't. But I will, anyway." She stops next to Mary and

83

runs her fingers along the silver necklace at the girl's throat. "These trinkets will sting if you get out of line, but they'll be nothing compared to the pain you'll suffer in the Rectory." She walks back down the row, slowly now, as if savoring every wince on our faces. "The few of you who've been there know what happens behind those walls." She stops next to me, her gaze cold. "Did you enjoy your stay, Delilah?"

I shake my head and ignore the phantom drip of water on my forehead. "No," my voice barely makes it past my lips.

"I didn't think so." She smiles. "But look at you now. Made holy in the sight of the Prophet."

I'm wearing a revealing white dress, the top dipping low between my breasts, and the hem barely covering my ass. At least they gave us white thongs to wear beneath them. With no bras, our tops are practically see-through. Dressed alike and each of us with makeup and overdone hair, we look the farthest thing from holy. I suppose the white hooker heels we're wearing lift us closer to heaven.

"Chastity," she barks, her eyes still on me. "Bring the robes."

Chastity emerges from the hallway, several white robes over her arm. More Spinners walk in, some with veils. They dress each of us, and I sigh with relief once I'm covered with the opaque fabric that buttons tightly at the neck and falls all the way to my ankles. The lacy veil gives me just enough vision and the fleeting feeling that I'm hidden. The clothes are uncomfortable, but at least I don't feel so exposed.

"We're ready." Grace finally leaves my side and heads to the front of the line. "Let's go."

The bus ride through the compound is a blur as Eve huddles next to me, her wide eyes holding more fear than I've ever seen. Perhaps she's mirroring me. The same worry that consumes her gnaws at my gut, too. A million questions flit through my mind about what's going to happen tonight. But no one will answer them for me. Instead, I focus on the few things I can control. Getting to Chastity is at the top of my list. She knows about Georgia and may be the key to me finding the killer. I won't be distracted from my primary mission again. Georgia is the only constant in my life—but that's the way it's always been.

"Girls!" My thoughts are derailed when the bus stops and Grace stands at the front. "Remember, best behavior."

We nod, and she turns and steps off the bus. Chastity waves for the rest of us to follow.

"I don't think I can." Eve's voice trembles at my ear. "I can't. I can't."

I take Eve's cold hand in mine, our touch hidden by the thick fabric of our robes. "You can."

"No." Tears roll down her cheeks, mascara streaking like the roots of a black tree.

The Maidens ahead of us stand and move down the aisle.

"Eve, you must." I grip her hand tighter and pull her to her feet.

"I just want to go back to my room. Just leave me

there." Her pleading rips at my heart, but there's nothing I can do.

"We have to move, Eve. I'll stay close to you for as long as I can, but we can't stay here."

"No." She yanks my hand with surprising strength. "I won't."

The aisle is cleared out, and we're the only ones left. A Spinner stands at the front of the bus, her focus on us. "Come on. Let's go."

"Eve, please," I hiss.

"I can't." The fracture in her voice matches the one in her mind. Gone is the girl who tried to escape, who fought for her freedom.

"Eve—" I'm cut off by a vicious sting at my throat, and Eve yelps.

The Spinner at the head of the bus motions, one of the control fobs in her hand. "There's more where that came from if you don't get moving."

I instinctively reach for the necklace, but it stings again. Clenching my eyes shut against the pain, I pull Eve along with me. She's full-on crying now, her fear coming out in heaving sobs.

"Stop your whimpering." The Spinner holds up the silver remote with several buttons, each one with a name beside it. "You're only going to make it worse."

I turn and face Eve. "We have to do this. Nothing bad will happen to us in front of the Heavenly crowd, okay? The Prophet just wants to show us off. That's all. Nothing bad will happen, okay?"

"I can't." She shakes her head.

"Maiden." The Spinner's warning tone raises the hackles on my neck, but I ignore her and focus on Eve.

"You can." I lift Eve's veil, turn my sleeve inside out, and use it to wipe her face clean. "We'll do it together. Come on. We have to go." Once the mascara streaks are gone, I lead her down the steps and out into the cold night, fully expecting another stinging blast from the cross around my neck, but none comes. The Spinner is probably just glad to be rid of us.

"Let's go." I keep hold of Eve's hand as we hurry to catch up to the line of Maidens. Our heels are loud on the black pavement, and we pass several cars parked along both sides of the narrow road. Glancing back, I find the Spinner at our backs, remote control still in hand. Of course.

We fall in line with the other Maidens, the Spinners surrounding us on all sides. We're a white column, moving slowly forward, scraping along the earth toward whatever murky fate the Prophet has in mind. Despite what I told Eve, I have no delusions that this night will come without peril.

A few churchgoers give us a wide berth as they hurry up the slight rise and join the swollen crowd that surrounds an enormous stack of wood. I gaze upward, trying to find the top of it against the inky night sky, but my eye can't capture the pinnacle.

"Eyes down," a Spinner hisses at my side.

I drop my gaze earthward and listen to the conversations going on around us. Most of them are planning their Christmas dinners or talking about relatives coming to visit—leading normal lives. Others discuss their intentions to move onto the compound and avoid the vile sinners of the world. I'd like to inform them that *they* are the sinners, but I don't want to think about the shock I'd receive if I did so.

We file upward until the ground evens out and we step off onto a damp, grassy path. Large white tents are set up around the outer perimeter of the clearing, and two firetrucks are parked amongst the trees. We keep walking to a wide wooden pavilion. Twelve white chairs are set up along the front, with several rows of benches behind them. Tables are arranged farther back, and hundreds of people are already seated while others move in orderly lines toward the open spots. Children play chase, darting through the throng, their laughter a discordant scratch on my ears. I can't tell if the women are just dressed for the cold, but the long skirts and complete absence of pants tells me that it isn't a coincidence. The Prophet's teaching has filtered through all the faithful, and the women are falling in line on their own or, more likely, being forced to. The sheer number of them wearing sunglasses at night is a good indicator.

I should be shocked at how easy it is for the Prophet to control thousands of people with nothing more than words. But I'm not. After all, he controls me too.

We're led to our chairs. The cold wood sends a shiver up my spine, the thick fabric of the robe doing nothing to stop the chill. Eve trembles beside me and keeps her head down, the veil hiding her from view. I peek up at the small stage set at the front of the pavilion. The Prophet's perch, no doubt. Other pavilions decorated with Christmas swags circle the huge wooden tower, each of them already filled to capacity with congregants spilling out the sides. The Heavenly Police force creates a wide perimeter around the center, guiding wayward children away from the structure whenever they venture too close. Even the little girls seem to be wearing long dresses, no pants to fight the lurking cold of this starless night.

I tuck my hands into my sleeves and close my eyes. Georgia appears again. Whole this time, young and beautiful—the way she'll always be in my memory.

Georgia flops down onto my bed and yelps.

"What?" I sit at my computer desk and try to write a paper on criminal psychology.

"How do you sleep on this?" She smacks the mattress.

I shrug. "I like it."

She lays on her back, her gold hair spilling across my rumpled bedspread. "It's torture."

"It's better than what I have at home."

"Oh." She reaches out and grabs my elbow, a look of sincere concern on her face. "Sorry. I didn't mean to say—"

"No, it's okay." I don't like talking about what life is like back at my mom's house. Not anymore. The drugs have made visits unbearable. She'd sold my bedroom set, so whenever I'd go for the weekend, I'd sleep on the same lumpy couch we'd had since I was five.

"Really." She squeezes my arm. "You know I love you."

"Of course." I give up on my paper and plop down

next to her, both of us staring at the water stains on the ceiling. "I'm just glad you came to visit."

"Me too. Are you going with me to Heavenly in the morning?"

"Hell no." I crinkle my nose at the thought.

"Why not?" She smacks my arm.

"I don't believe in any of that. And the Prophet creeps me out."

She smacks me harder. "You're going to hell for that."

I laugh. "Tell me something I don't know."

"Don't you think he's handsome? A total silver fox." Her voice goes dreamy. "And you can just tell he talks to God."

"No one talks to God."

"He does."

"No, he probably just talks to himself. He definitely thinks he's a god."

She giggles. "Blasphemy."

"Pfft. He's just a man, like any other man. Don't fall for that nonsense."

"I'm not falling for anything." She shrugs. "I believe. You have to have faith, you know?"

"I do have faith. In me. In you. And that's about it."

She sighs. "Well, as long as you believe in me, I guess that's okay."

"Thanks for the permission. And I'm beginning to suspect you only come visit me so you can see your silver fox prophet."

"What?" She waves a delicate hand in the air, swatting the idea away like it's a gnat. "Of course not! I also come so I can compare Alabama parties versus LSU parties."

I snort. "You're such a bitch."

She laughs, the strength of it shaking the bed and loosening my tightly-bound soul. "I know. But you still love me."

I roll my eyes. "Well, what's the verdict? Which parties do you like better?"

"Alabama is fun and all, but I prefer LSU."

"Why?"

She shrugs. "I think the booze is better somehow?"

"Bad girl." I'm not much for parties. Really, I only go whenever Georgia is in town. Even then, I stick to the wall, religiously guarding my drink and hers the entire time while she dances and flirts.

"Not bad enough." She sighs. "I still have the v-card."

"You better still have it." I elbow her. "That's a definite phone call sort of thing."

"I couldn't just text you about it?" I can hear the smile in her voice.

"Texting is like breathing for you. You text me when you sneeze or when you see a butterfly or when you're on the can. No—news like that deserves a phone call."

"Having to call someone on the phone is enough of a deterrent that I'll never want to lose my virginity. What about you?"

I wriggle away from her. "What about me? I'm not allergic to talking on the phone like you are."

"You know what I mean." She rolls over so she's lying half on top of me, her Bath and Body Works scent as familiar as my own reflection. "Have you met the right guy yet?"

"Get off." I playfully shove her aside, and we settle down next to each other again, the afternoon sun striping through my blinds. "And no. I don't have time for guys. Double majoring in criminology and psychology doesn't leave much room for anything else."

"You have time for me." She twines her pinky finger with mine.

"Always. That's what sisters are for, right?"

CHAPTER 12

ADAM

The masses have assembled, each one of them aching for a show—the sort only their Prophet can provide. I check with Tony on the final preparations for the bonfire, then head toward the main pavilion.

The snow white line of Maidens at the front draws my eye, and I focus on Delilah. She looks straight ahead, but she's not there. Lost in thought, she doesn't see me approach. I stride onto the pavilion steps and tilt my chin at Noah who leans against the support post at the side. My father will make his grand entry there and greet his fans with an enthusiastic—and hopefully brief—Christmas Eve message.

Grace and a host of Spinners wait on the other side of the pavilion, their eyes on the Maidens.

A few churchgoers who don't know any better greet me with handshakes and smiles. I return them, but something always dies in their eyes once they get a closer look at mine. Good.

I sidle over to Noah. "Ready to get going?"

"Yeah. I want to see some shit burn."

I don't comment on the whiskey on his breath. There's no point. And, given our circumstances, I don't blame him.

I focus my attention on Delilah, her veil hiding most of her profile from me. I want to rip that stupid bit of lace away and study her, see what's going on inside. But I'm kidding myself. She keeps secrets from me—ones I'll get out of her in time.

"Here we go." Noah jerks his chin as my father appears at the side of the pavilion, a broad smile on his face.

"Welcome!" His voice booms as he shakes hands and manages to kiss a baby on his way to the podium.

Applause spreads through the pavilions until the din rises into the sky and dies far short of heaven. Dad casts a glance at the Maidens, then turns to address the crowd. Just holding up one of his hands stops the roar of appreciation. The big-screen TVs flicker on in each of the pavilions, my father's face smiling down at all of Heavenly Ministries—including locations all over the United States and the world. Cameramen disperse through the crowd, shooting the happy churchgoers to beam into the homes of the faithful. I stifle an eye roll.

"My sacred children, welcome!"

Another roar from the sycophants tramples the air. Movement behind my father draws my eye. My mother moves silently, her head down, her face covered with a black veil.

"Hey." I elbow Noah.

He looks and stiffens. "Does she seem okay?"

She walks with her usual limp, but nothing else seems amiss. Castro is at her side, his beady eyes surveying the crowd as he helps her to a black chair far to the side of the podium. He doesn't manhandle her the same way he does in my father's presence. I ignore this detail and focus on the fact that several goons are missing.

"Where are the rest?" I scan the area for my mother's usual guards, but I can't see them.

Noah stops leaning against the pillar. "They have to be here somewhere, but I don't see them."

My thoughts fire in rapid succession, creating a plan. Once the bonfire is going, all eyes will be on the flames.

I edge closer to Noah. "We can get her out this time."

His eyes widen. "We can't."

"We can. I'll take care of Castro. You grab her. I'll grab Delilah."

He glances around. "There's too many people."

"We wait until they're dismissed." I try to think ahead, to plan each step and take into account what happens when shit goes south. Our chances of success are slim—but if there's a possibility I can save my mother and Delilah from my father's cruelty, I have to try. "Then we make our move. If it's just Castro, we can do this." Other Protectors are sprinkled in the crowd, but I'll do whatever I have to if that means freedom. "I'll clear a path for us. But I need you onboard. All right?"

A memory of the last time flits through my vision. He agreed then, and we almost made it out. But that 'almost' led to some of the oldest scars on my back and our mother's broken leg. He's replaying it, too. I can tell from the way he tenses.

"Noah, we can do this, okay? This time—"

"This time what?" He keeps his voice low, but there's anger in it. "We won't get busted? Mom won't get tortured right in front of us?"

I'm losing him. *Fuck.* Desperation dries my throat, and I swallow hard. "Noah, I can't do this without you. We have to work together—"

"No way. Castro will kill her before you get the chance to do anything. And what about Dad?" His eyes burn into mine, as if he already knows my plans for our father. And maybe he does.

"Don't worry about that. I'll do what I have to do."

"No." He shakes his head minutely. "I won't risk Mom."

"Noah—"

"I said no!" Noah's yell catches too much attention.

I step away from him as eyes turn toward us, and my father stops in the middle of whatever nonsense he's spouting. He casts me a glare, then replaces it with his usual smile before continuing. Eventually, people stop looking and the crowd begins to hum amongst themselves.

Noah crosses his arms over his chest. I've lost him. Either to whiskey, his fear, or his delusions about our father. Disappointment slams me back to earth, my plans disappearing like fog under the harsh light of day. Even now, I can't blame Noah, can't seem to convict him for his treason, because I truly believe that he just can't fucking help it. That knowledge doesn't ease my desire to make a move against my father, but it certainly crushes any chances of success. Even so, I keep an eye on my mother, always alert for an opportunity to end this nightmare for all of us.

My father steps onto the podium. "We are blessed to be here to celebrate the birth of our Lord and Savior. He is the reason for this season of giving and love. He is the salvation that leads us through this life and into the next. Just as you believe in me, you must believe in Him, for God has anointed us both—one as His son and another as his holy prophet."

More clapping erupts, along with hallelujahs shouted here and there.

Half a dozen men walk past us, the rest of my father's guard contingent, and take position along the rail next to my mother.

Noah glances at me, but I don't look at him. Whatever "I told you so" he's trying to convey can't erase his cowardice for refusing to even *try* for freedom. I may not blame him for it, but I won't forget it.

My father drones on for another ten minutes or so as I scan the crowd, my gaze always drawn back to Delilah. She's covered in white from head to toe—the picture of modesty. But that won't last. The night is young, and the Prophet will show his lambs to their best advantage.

My hackles rise as the senator from earlier walks along the far aisle, his gaze sweeping over the row of Maidens and landing unerringly on Delilah. He stops just behind her and sits in a reserved seat. Leaning forward, he whispers something to her. She turns her head, and my blood begins to pound in my temples.

He reaches toward her veil. I take a step forward. When his fingers brush the lace, I tense and calculate how quickly I can launch myself across the pews full of adoring idiots.

"Whoa." Noah grabs my arm, his grip firm. "Don't move."

"Get off me."

"You're about to get yourself into the worst trouble of your life." Despite the liquor on his breath, his words are accurate.

"—and now we will light the bonfire and lift our voices to the heavens." My father turns toward the massive structure, and everyone in the pavilion stands.

I break away from Noah's grip. His fingers grasp at my suit coat, but I'm already darting away, heading straight for Delilah and the asshole who thinks he can talk to her.

The whoosh of flames steals my breath, and the breaths of everyone around me. I stop and stare as the massive tower lights from the base, the gasoline quickly burning away as the flames race to the top. It's a hellish Christmas tree, the orange glow lighting the night sky. The wood creaks and groans as it's swallowed up by the inferno, and a wave of heat blasts the crowd. A collective gasp leads to whooping and cheering. No matter how "holy" these people believe they are, they're standing next to a raging fire and howling into the night like primitive man.

"For the glory of God!" My father's voice booms over the speakers as a cameraman slowly circles the bonfire, his images appearing on the TVs.

Ash begins to float through the air, some of it carrying glowing embers. My amazement fades, and I redouble my efforts to get to Delilah.

"Boss! I mean, Adam!" Someone yells from behind me. I glance over my shoulder. Tony pushes through the crowd, relief crossing his strained face when he sees me. "Boss—"

"I'm busy." I turn my back and step over a pew. Hurting the senator in full view of everyone isn't an option, but if I can talk him into stepping away to chat with me—maybe lure him with talk of Delilah—then what happens next will be worth whatever lashes my father decides to lay on me.

"Wait." Tony follows. "Boss, the main fire hose is jammed."

"What?" I'd arranged the Heavenly Fire Department around the outskirts so they could spray the pavilion roofs to keep the structures safe.

"It's jammed." He pulls a grimy handkerchief from his back pocket and wipes his brow.

"Did you wet the roofs before like I told you?"

"Yes, sir." He swipes his neck. "Except one."

"What?"

"It jammed right before we could spray the main children's pavilion around the back side. We've been trying to..." He keeps yammering as I notice several people nearby, their ears cocked to listen though they don't meet my eye.

I yank Tony by the arm and pull him away before he starts a panic. Problem is, this leads me away from Delilah and the senator. But I have to choose.

Embers swirl through the air, ones that could easily send the children's pavilion up in flames. The senator leans closer, his silver tongue in Delilah's ear. I want to rip him apart, but I can't. Not now. I turn on my heel and stride out into the night.

It burns—sears my fucking flesh—to walk away from Delilah. But one thought of my sweet Faith tells me that I'm choosing correctly. What if she were in that pavilion?

"Come on." I pull off my jacket as Tony and I hurry away toward the fire truck parked amongst the trees. "Let's get to work."

I barely feel the hilt of the pistol as it crashes into the back of my skull.

CHAPTER 13

DELILAH

*H*is sermon over and sealed with a prayer, the Prophet waves at his faithful as the inferno burns, the flames at the top still high, the sides smoldering with deep orange embers. "Go now, under the light of a loving God and with the blessing of your Prophet."

"Amen!" ricochets around the clearing, and the crowd begins to disperse. The Heavenly police officers help herd the mass of people away from the fire and toward the road. I take a chance to look around for Adam, but he's not here. Tamping down my disappointment, I survey the rest of the pavilion.

Senator Roberts still hovers at my back, but now he's speaking to someone else. I want to shrink, to disappear into nothing so he won't notice me anymore, but I can tell that isn't going to happen.

"I like you in white," he'd whispered as the Prophet gave his Christmas Eve sermon.

My skin crawls, and I take deep breaths to calm myself. Eve's fingers graze my leg, and I grab her hand, keeping the forbidden bit of comfort hidden beneath the voluminous robes.

Glancing to the side, I see Adam's mother rising from her chair and being escorted away by several armed men. What does she think of this pageantry, of the filthy empire her husband has created?

I get out of my own head and squeeze Eve's fingers. "Everything's going to be okay."

She doesn't respond but leans into me a bit. A little girl of no more than five walks down the row of Maidens, her eyes wide as she inspects us. I try to imagine what we look like to her. Creepy maybe? A line of ghosts with shattered souls hidden beneath white veils?

Her mother, wearing a dress that almost touches the floor, walks up and takes her hand. "Come on, baby."

The girl resists her mother's pull, her big brown eyes focused on me. "Can I be a Maiden one day?"

My stomach churns, and I fight the urge to dry heave.

The mother leans down. "If you are faithful and obedient, you may be chosen by the Prophet."

The girl nods. "I will be. And then I can be a Maiden, too."

Not if I can help it. Just looking at her angelic face and bright eyes changes something inside me. I watch her walk away, hand in hand with her mother, her steps light. I came here for Georgia, knowing it was too late to save her. She was dead and gone, vengeance my only mission. But watching that little girl, seeing hope in her eyes—the false hope put there by the Prophet—I realize that maybe Georgia led me here to do more than just avenge her death. Maybe I'm here to end this place—not for revenge, but to save any more girls from going through this hell.

"Delilah!"

I snap my head up and find Grace standing in front of me. "Yes?"

She bobbles the remote in her hand, her face pinched. "I was speaking to you. Senator Roberts would like to meet with you now."

Breaking my grip on Eve, I stand and follow Grace around the last Heavenly stragglers. The senator waits against the far rail, a grin on his handsome face.

I keep my steps steady as my hands break out into a clammy sweat.

"We're clear!" someone yells. Several shouts of "clear" ring out, and a low steady beat begins to play through the sound system. Servers appear from the tents set up at the rear of the pavilions, scurrying out with trays of drinks and food. Protectors and dozens of men—suitors, I assume—remain.

Grace pulls off my veil, then works the robe buttons at my throat. I'm exposed, and there's nowhere to hide from the senator's too-interested gaze. Protectors and attendants stack up the pews and place them outside the pavilion, then replace them with plush chairs and couches.

She strips the robe off, and the blast of cool air chills my skin. My nipples harden embarrassingly, and I know the senator notices, because he licks his lips. A waft of warmth from the bonfire mixes with the chilly night, alternating hot and cold along my exposed body.

"Nice to finally meet you. Formally, I mean." He holds out a hand.

Grace pushes me in the lower back, forcing me closer to him. "Best behavior," she whispers.

I take his hand to shake, but he pulls me to him until we're almost touching. The heels help, but I still have to tilt my chin up to catch his eyes.

"I'm Evan." He doesn't release my hand.

"Delilah."

"What's your real name?" His cologne is expensive, sophisticated and with subtle notes I can't follow.

"Delilah." I'm desperate to rip my hand away from his, but the heavy necklace around my throat reminds me that anything I do will have consequences—bad ones.

"That's how you're going to play it, *Delilah*?" One side of his lips quirk. He'd be handsome if I didn't know what a horrible, ghoulish soul lives inside of him.

"I'm not playing anything." I silently scream for Adam to appear, to do something, anything to get me out of this man's grasp.

"We'll see." He glances at my lips.

I lean back instinctively, and he laughs, a deep-throated sound that raises the hair along the back of my neck.

"This is going to be a fun little chase, isn't it?" He leans closer, invading my space. "Even though we both know it's going to end with you tied to my bed for however long I want."

"Fuck you." I don't think about the words before they spill out.

His eyes widen. "Oh, Delilah. I like that very much." He pulls my unwilling hand to his crotch so I can feel his growing erection. "I love the ones that fight."

"Yeah?" I grip his dick hard.

He yells, and the shock at my neck makes me stagger backwards.

"Delilah!" Grace rushes over and grabs me by the hair. "I'm so sorry, Senator. This one is willful to the point that she needs additional—"

"It's fine." Evan holds up a hand and uses the other to adjust himself in his pants. "Completely fine. In fact, I'd like to discuss this little wildcat with the Prophet sooner rather than later."

Grace pulls my hair harder, and I have to arch my back to keep the follicles from ripping away. Evan peruses my body with open lust, and I consider throwing an elbow to escape Grace's grip. But that would only lead to more pain for me. Not escape. Never that.

"Let her go." He ices his tone, and Grace reluctantly obeys, loosening her hold.

I sidestep her and cross my arms over my chest as a chunk of the bonfire structure crashes in on itself, sending a rush of heat blowing past and fading cinders floating through the air.

"I'd like you to put her robe back on." He finally releases me from his gaze and turns to Grace.

"I'm afraid that's not possible. The Maidens have

been specially prepared for the evening." Grace shakes her head.

"I don't want anyone else looking at her." He moves toward Grace, who, to my shock, takes a step back.

His proprietary tone sets my teeth on edge. I'm not some toy that he can buy. Then again, I remind myself, that's exactly what I am—one of the Prophet's whores that he will sell to whomever pays the most.

Grace stands firm this time. "I understand, but until we have a completed arrangement between you and the Prophet, Delilah belongs to Heavenly, and the Prophet will do with her as he sees fit."

He clenches his jaw. "Take me to him."

"Again, I can't do that. He's about to begin his—"

"Welcome to the real celebration!" The Prophet walks around the bonfire, his crimson robe flecked with gold.

Grace takes me by the elbow and leads me away, Evan's gaze heavy on my back. She laughs a little. "Anticipation will make him even more desperate. And then, once he offers the right price, I'll be rid of you." She shoves me back into my chair. "Stay here until it's time."

Time for what? I don't ask. She wouldn't tell me anyway. Instead, she wanders off among the hungry suitors, some of them forming circles around the Maidens.

The Prophet's voice booms through the sound system. "The winter solstice is finally upon us, a time when we celebrate the gifts of our Heavenly Father as well as those from the Father of Fire!"

I glance at the people gathered nearby. Not one of

them bats an eyelash when the Prophet mentions what I can only assume is the devil. One of the suitors strikes up a conversation with Evan, but he keeps an eye on me. I wish for my robe and veil.

"This year there is much to celebrate, my friends. A beautiful crop of Maidens, the expansion of our Ministry, and the beginning of Monroeville. I'd like to thank all of you for coming and making our mission possible." He walks toward my pavilion, the fire raging at his back. Despite the possibility of the structure falling over and crushing him with flames, he isn't afraid. "As a reward, I offer you this free access to my blessed Maidens, as well as other delights."

At his word, several nude women file out of the tents set up behind the pavilions. I recognize a few faces from the Chapel, but they look through me. Drugged and empty, they strut into the crowd of suitors.

"Indulge, and let your celebrations be in the name of your Prophet."

I turn to face him, refusing to watch the scene behind me as it devolves into debauchery.

"Maidens, come to me, your father." He catches my eye and motions to me.

The necklace at my throat tingles, a reminder to comply. I'm not the only one who feels it, since Maidens file past me toward him, and I join.

A braying noise cuts through the sound of talking, and a Spinner leads a lamb through the clearing toward the Prophet.

I swallow hard. Adam always calls me "little lamb."

As I see the true embodiment of his words, a deep foreboding falls over me. It "baas" again and lets the Spinner lead it toward the charlatan in the crimson robe.

"On your knees," Grace hisses and pushes me down in front of the Prophet. All the Maidens drop in a line as the Spinner holds the lamb nearby. It's still somewhat small, not quite an adult. Its dark eyes don't seem to focus on anything in particular, and I almost envy how oblivious it is.

"The Book of Leviticus tells us 'you must sacrifice as a burnt offering to the Lord a lamb a year old without defect.'" The Prophet pulls a long, curved knife from his robe. "And the Father of Fire loves nothing more than the pleasing smells of freshly-spilled blood and roasting meat."

The Spinner grabs the animal's chin and lifts it sharply, its throat exposed. It shifts on its feet but doesn't complain.

Run. The word is on repeat in my mind as I will the sacrifice to flee and save itself. My silent request doesn't stop the Prophet's blade. The lamb protests then falls silent as its blood spurts to the ground and its legs give way. I can't feel anything, my body going silent as I watch this needless slaughter. Deep red stains the innocent white fleece, the Prophet's violence tainting even the purest of creatures.

Someone grabs the shoulders of my dress and rips it down. Other Spinners do the same down the line until the Maidens are nude except for the skimpy thongs. The

Prophet speaks in a language I've never heard, then dips his hands in the lamb's blood.

"For you are chosen." He starts at the end of the row and rubs his bloodied hands on Eve's chest. "Precious to your Prophet." He continues down the line, and when he gets to me, he uses fresh blood. It's still warm, and the unmistakable tang of copper fills my nose as he paints me with his mark of evil. "You will live forever in the light of my love."

When he's done, the Spinners get us up and herd us back to the pavilion where the suitors engage in carnal acts with the girls from the Chapel, or stare, transfixed, as the nude, bloodied Maidens return.

The fire intensifies, a wave of heat at my back like a sunburn.

"The Father of Fire is pleased!" the Prophet crows.

A suitor has a woman bent over my chair, her breasts bouncing as he rams her from behind. I don't look in her dead eyes. Instead, I turn to watch the Prophet. He raises his bloodied hands to the sky. "Bring her!"

My breath freezes in my lungs as a Spinner shoves a woman into the clearing, her steps uneven, her body bloody and carved with a roadmap of runes and religious symbols.

I rush to the pavilion railing, but the sting at my neck tells me I can go no farther. "Sarah!"

CHAPTER 14

ADAM

Castro smacks me across the face. "Wake up, *pendejo*."

I've been awake for about thirty seconds, trying to figure out what the hell is going on while pretending to be out. Bound tightly to a chair, I've only been able to discern that Tony is scared of what will happen when I wake, Castro is excited, and there are at least a half dozen other men around me in the small tent. Opening my eyes, I stare at Castro, then train my gaze on my mother.

She sits across from me, defeated, her eyes watery.

"What the fuck?" I strain against the duct tape but get nowhere.

Tony shrinks back against the white flap of the tent when I turn my ire on him. "The fuck, Tony?"

"Shut up." Castro grabs my mother by the hair. "Or she gets hurt."

Fire leaps through my veins and I pull harder at the tape. It doesn't budge.

"What the fuck is this?"

Castro smiles. "The Prophet has a special plan for you tonight. He's been worried you aren't on the same page, aren't a believer."

I spit on the floor. "No one does more for Heavenly than I do."

Castro's eyes narrow. "You spoiled piece of shit. You don't deserve to have the same blood as your father."

I laugh. "Sucking Dad's dick sure has made you bold."

A few of the men around me snort back a laugh. Castro pulls my mother's head to the side. She doesn't cry out. Violence doesn't faze her anymore.

"Shut your lying mouth." He taps the butt of his gun beneath his suit coat. "Or I'll shut it for you."

"Is there a point?" I let my head loll back with feigned boredom. My father's voice subsided a while ago, the throng of Heavenly worshippers getting into their warm cars and heading home.

"It's time," someone from outside calls.

Castro smirks. "Cut loose his feet but not his hands."

Gray leans down and cuts my ankles free. I jerk my knee up and nail him in the face out of nothing more than spite. He squeals and falls backward onto his ass, then grabs his bloody nose with one hand.

"Sorry man. Reflexes." I grin down at him as another Protector yanks me to my feet.

"Keep it up." Castro whips out his pistol and points it at me.

I glance at Mom. They aren't dragging her up—a

relief. And Castro has already let go of her hair. Maybe they're done with her for the evening.

"Come on." Castro grabs one of my elbows.

Another Protector reaches for my mother, but Castro barks, "Stop." He shoves me out of the tent's door. "I'll be back for her later."

Fuck.

He marches me through the night and around to the bonfire. A dead lamb lies in the clearing, and my father lifts his crimson hands high above his head. A girl kneels in front of him—the one that led the escape attempt. Sarah, I think is her name.

I instinctively look for Delilah. She's standing in the pavilion. Red blood paints her chest, and she grips the rail as Castro pushes me toward my father and Sarah.

My father greets me with a glare. "Adam, my first-born, has sinned against me."

No shit.

Castro shoves me until I'm standing next to my father, then cuts my hands free. He backs away, apparently satisfied that I won't make a move. The other Protectors fan out.

The crowd at Delilah's back is engaged in acts of depravity—the Chapel girls serving as the evening's entertainment for all the suitors. Some of them glance at the scene my father is creating, but most of them are too busy with the delights of the flesh to bother.

My mother isn't spared. Castro pulls her to the edge of the clearing, his blade at her throat and a Protector on either side of him. Noah busts through the crowd and rushes past Delilah. He jumps the steps to the ground, but Gray and Zion close in on him and stop him from getting any closer. Gray pulls his pistol and presses it against Noah's ribs.

My father continues, "Adam, who I created from my own heart and soul, schemes against me, defies me, and seeks to undermine me at every opportunity. The Father of Fire has revealed his iniquity to me and given me this one chance to bring him back into the fold." He hands me the bloody, curved blade. I take it and imagine slicing through his neck, pouncing on him as he struggles, and sawing all the way through his spinal column. But the knife at my mother's throat and the gun trained on Noah keep me frozen. Just as they always have.

Sarah, her battered body and face covered with blood, sways fervently at my father's feet. Her mouth moves with silent words, her pupils huge and black.

"The Father of Fire seeks to bless us this coming year —more than He ever has." The flames jump higher behind my father, the heat pressing against my back.

Delilah and Noah raise their gazes, and I turn to see a tornado of fire twisting around the smoldering pile of wood and ash.

"But He must first receive a greater gift—one that far exceeds the life of a simple animal. For Him to bless us, He requires the ultimate sacrifice."

"I'm ready!" Sarah cries and presses her forehead to the dirt. Her emaciated body is weak and wan in the orange glow, and I can feel the emptiness inside her.

"For you, Prophet. For you!" She stretches her arms along the ground in a gesture of total obedience.

My blood runs cold, and I no longer feel the heat from the fire. I don't look at Noah or my mother. My gaze travels to Delilah's. Her eyes are wide. Gray—his nose still bloody—walks up behind her, grabs her around the waist, and presses a long hunting knife to her throat.

Bending down, my father coaxes Sarah into a sitting position. "Chosen girl, my favorite of all my Maidens. Are you ready to please me?"

"Anything. Please. I'll do it for you." Her pupils are wide black holes of nothing as she stares at my father with adoration. "Let me serve you."

"Of course, my child." He grabs her hair and gently tilts her chin up. "You will be the first to serve me in paradise."

She clutches his leg as he turns and gives me a hard stare.

"For the glory of the Father of Fire, this is what you must do, Adam. If you wish to become the man I know you can be—the one to inherit all I have built here—you must fall in line. You must declare your obedience to me as your Prophet. Like the wayward Prodigal Son, you must repent. 'Bring the fattened calf and kill it.' This is the word of our Lord. And you must follow it and submit to me."

The wooden hilt of the blade warms in my hand, and I look at Delilah. Her eyes beg me to stop, to be the man and not the monster. Even when there's a knife at her throat, Delilah would make the right decision. That's what separates us. I've never made the right choice.

Noah throws an elbow and tries to run to me, but Zion grabs his collar as Gray pistol whips him. He falls in a heap as they continue beating him.

My father tosses away his mic. "Do you want them to stop? Do you want your mother to take another breath? Do you want your Maiden to take you in her ass again?" He shakes Sarah. "Then do it. Make this sacrifice or I'll bury you on the same hill as your bastard daughter, right along with your mother and your brother. I have plenty more children."

I grip the hilt hard and step toward him. It would be so easy to end him, to put a stop to all of this.

"She's innocent." I stare at the smooth lines of her throat and the bloody cross on the center of her chest.

"She's been claimed by the Prophet. Not innocent, but holy. And the Father of Fire demands her sacrifice. I have seen his many blessings, Adam. He will bless you, too. And you will rule at my side."

She trembles. "Please, let me serve the Prophet."

I shake my head. "You don't want this."

"Think of your brother." His voice slithers around me like the caress of Death.

Noah is face down now. Zion and Gray kick his limp body as hard as they can. He won't be able to withstand it for long.

I look at Delilah, staring into her eyes. I can't tell her I'm sorry. But I need her to know. I need her to know that I've buried her hope for me down deep, away from the death and the blood. I've put it somewhere that it can grow if she'll only let her light shine on me again.

As I press the blade to Sarah's neck and her blood spurts onto my hands, I don't bother asking God to forgive me. Nothing will ever wipe away this stain.

CHAPTER 15

DELILAH

*M*y scream comes from somewhere deep, a well of grief that I didn't know existed. It explodes from inside me in shades of agony as I crumple to my knees. The other Maidens gasp and some wail, but I can't focus on anything except the blood. A river of it pouring onto Adam's hands and the ground as Sarah's soul flies free from her battered body.

The fire intensifies, the tornado of sparks and flames widening as the Prophet faces the inferno with arms raised.

Adam kneels beside Sarah and catches her before she slumps to the ground. He holds her in his arms like a broken doll. He bows his head, his shoulders hunched. I can't blink, can't do anything except stare at the gore, at the man who murdered my friend right in front of me. Everything is cold. Every ounce of heat evaporates as the fire—a raging inferno only moments ago—lessens into nothing more than a smoldering heap.

Huge gasping sobs wrack my body, and I can't begin to deal with the enormity of the emotions that rip and tear through my heart. Adam doesn't move as the Prophet dips his hands in Sarah's blood and paints Adam's face with streaks of crimson. Then the Prophet does the same to his own cheeks, drawing his cruelty in the deepest shades of red.

Georgia. Was it Adam who did the same to her? I can see her instead of Sarah, my beautiful sister limp in Adam's strong arms, her blood a river.

Something drapes over my shoulders, and I'm scooped off the floor. Evan holds me to his chest, his jacket wrapped around me.

"Let me go." I'm paralyzed. So much inside me died right along with Sarah.

"I think you're safer here." He tightens his grip.

I turn back to Adam, to the innocent blood that saturates his clothes, his skin, his soul. A tremor shakes me, my teeth chattering. "H-he killed her."

The Prophet approaches, a rapturous look on his bloody face. "The faithful will be rewarded. All of you." He waves to the orgy going on behind me. "The Lord shines on us as his chosen, and each of us will reap the benefits." He turns his gaze to me. "And what do we have here?"

Grace scampers to Evan's side. "I told him to stop taking liberties with Delilah, but he—"

The Prophet waves a dismissive hand. "It's all right, as long as she's still intact?" He raises his eyebrows in question.

Grace nods.

"Very good." He ignores me and addresses Evan. "Of course, you can't take her with you. She belongs to me."

"I understand." Evan doesn't loosen his grip. "But I'd like to discuss her future with you as soon as possible."

The Prophet smiles, his evil horrible to behold. "We'll turn to business after the solstice is over. Until then, enjoy the finest the Chapel has to offer. But it's past my pure Maidens' bedtimes." He turns and waves one of the Protectors over. "Bring them."

The Protector hurries toward one of the far tents as my gaze strays back to Adam. He hasn't moved. My heart breaks and vibrates with fury all at once, and I can't decide if I want to kill him or heal him.

"I suppose this is goodnight then." Evan sighs and sets me on my feet.

My knees wobble, and black spots float across my vision, but I stay upright. I can't look at him. How can any human see something so horrible and not react? I'm surrounded by devils, and Evan is no different.

I shrug off his jacket.

"Keep it." He snugs it back around me. The scent of his cologne makes my stomach twist in an even tighter knot.

"I'm not yours." I finally look him in the eye.

He smiles ruefully, his blue eyes glinting. "Not *yet*."

"Girls!" Grace's shout shakes me out of the nightmare, but somehow also reinforces it. "Back to the bus."

I wobble on my heels but fall in line, shoving off Evan's jacket the moment I'm out of his grasp. Eve weeps in front of me, her bare shoulders shaking as we're led from the pavilion. Two Protectors grab Adam and yank him away from Sarah. Her lifeless body falls to the cold ground, and several of the Maidens scream.

A line of women—ones I've never seen before—and children walk in a line toward Sarah's body, the Prophet leading them. The women are in long dresses, their hair in tight buns. The children wear white jumpers, the same ones I've seen every Sunday. They all kneel, and the Prophet uses Sarah's blood to draw a cross on each of their foreheads.

They disappear from view as I'm herded down the empty road toward the white bus, the frigid air chilling my bare skin. Adam is gone, dragged away. Will I ever see him again? The question lingers, and I can't grasp the threads of our connection—not when I can see him holding Georgia the same way, her blood on his hands.

Back on the bus, we retrieve our robes. I wrap mine around me, not caring about the lamb's blood marring the fabric. I'm in a numb daze, too many feelings at war inside me, and a glaze of disbelief coating the top. Other than some sniffles, the ride is silent and somber, not even Grace uttering a word. I cry silently, the tears never-ending, the pain so dire that my eyes can't contain the grief.

We file into the Cloister and return to our rooms. I stare at Sarah's closed door across the hall. *She'll never come back.* The thought is as obvious as it is agonizing.

The pipes creak as the Maidens shower to wash off the blood. As if what happened tonight is something that could ever flow away down the drain. I'm still rooted in the hallway, staring at Sarah's door when Chastity hurries over to me. Another Spinner is in the hall, but she looks away as Chastity shuffles me into my room and closes the door.

"Were you there?" I let her strip the dirty robe off me.

"I'd already left. But I heard." She kneels and unstraps my heels, sliding them off one at a time, then guides me toward the bathroom and turns on the shower. "Get in."

I peel off the thong and step into the spray, my muscles on autopilot. "He killed her." The water hits my face and mingles with the tears. "Adam did it."

"I know." She soaps up a washcloth and washes my face first, then the rest of me.

"Did he do it. Before? To Georgia?" I ask the question that has terrified me since the first day I met him. "Was it him?"

She turns me so the spray hits my back. "No. At least I don't think so." Her voice is barely audible over the hiss of the water. "The Prophet has never done this before. At least, not openly. He sacrifices animals every year. It's part of his ritual to the Father of Fire. But he's never gone this far. Not even Grace knew what he had planned."

"Adam cut her throat." The words make it too real, and I sink to my knees. Chastity drops to the floor beside the tub and pushes the wet hair out of my face.

"It's going to be all right."

"How?" I look at her with the most honesty I've

shown to anyone since I've been at the Cloister. "How can any of this ever be all right?"

Her eyes water. "I don't know. But it will be. We'll make it all right. You, me, and some of the others." She takes a deep breath. "Okay, let's get you dry." She turns off the faucet and wraps me in a towel, then walks me to the bed.

"She had the same markings," I whisper. "The same as Georgia's body."

"They're from the Prophet's book."

"Book?"

"He has a book that he believes was dictated to him by the Father of Fire. I've never seen it. But my Protector told me about it when I was a Maiden. He said it has all sorts of symbols and crazy writing in it, and the Prophet believes it's a prophecy of the coming war between his people and the rest of the world." She glances at the door. "I have to go. I've used up all my favors with Spinner Bethlehem to get this time with you."

"If the Prophet is the only one with access to the book, then he must have been the one who ordered Georgia's death." I grab Chastity's hand. "Can you promise me it wasn't Adam? If he killed Georgia—"

"I can't promise, but I have reason to believe it was someone else." She pulls her hand free and backs to the door.

"Who?"

"Soon." She opens the door and slips out.

I climb into my bed, not bothering with the white dress. Curling into a ball, I can't stop the gruesome picture show in my mind. So much blood. And in the center of it, Adam.

Sarah didn't scream when the knife cut through her skin. My thoughts ricochet off each other. *Adam cut with a sure hand, as if he'd done it before.* The flames swirl at his back, urging him on. So many horrible memories pile onto each other that I suffocate beneath the weight.

Am I asleep, awake?

My skin tingles then heats until I feel as if I'm standing in front of the fire, the tornado whipping around and burning my flesh off with each twist of the flames. Fighting the towering inferno is impossible, but I hold my ground. I blister and scorch, the fire consuming me until nothing is left but singed bone and ash. When the fire relents, Adam appears through the smoke, his face covered in blood, and collects my remains as a trophy.

CHAPTER 16

ADAM

I sit in my shower, the walls and door shattered, glass all around me. Cold water pours onto me as I drink straight from the bottle I grabbed on my way up. Maybe Noah is onto something after all.

The Protectors dumped me on my front step, and one of them stayed to stand guard. I'm even more of a prisoner. So I sit and let the water run and drink myself into oblivion.

Noah won't be showing up to give me some words of comfort. I don't even know if he survived his beating. No one will tell me anything. I replay what I did over and over. How easily the metal cut through her skin, the warm blood spurting over my hands, the look of utter horror in Delilah's eyes as I became the monster she always feared.

I take another large swig from the bottle.

The water can't wash away my sins. Not this one, especially. That girl didn't deserve to die. I killed her. I didn't have to. I could have thrown the knife down, maybe even turned it on myself. Would it have saved my mother or Noah? No. Would Delilah also pay the price for my disobedience? Yes. But none of these explanations can erase the evil I committed tonight. A clock chimes midnight downstairs. Merry Fucking Christmas.

I stagger to my feet and sway out of my bathroom and into the hallway. Bloody footprints mark my progress, my feet slipping against the wood floor. The door across from mine is shut like always. I lean against it and press my forehead to the wood. I haven't been inside since the day she left, floating out of my life as I held her in my arms. Why do I keep failing her?

With a shaking hand, I turn the knob. The familiar scent of baby lotion still lingers. I stumble in and hit my knees on her rug, the rainbow colors bright despite the thin layer of dust. I rest my head on her little bed, the covers still rumpled from the last morning she woke up. My face is wet. And I know it isn't just from the shower. When Faith died, something inside me broke, and I knew it would never be repaired. But what I did tonight—it crushed what was left of me. I'm the husk my father always wanted, the empty vessel he can fill with his lies and hatred.

I can't get Delilah's horrified face out of my mind. She'll never forgive me. Not that I want to be forgiven. I've done so many terrible things. She was my last hope at redemption. A chance to change and become something more. But that's all gone now.

"I'm sorry." My voice is cracked and raw just like the

rest of me. But the words pour out and profane this holy space where my Faith lingers—in the indention on her pillow, the unicorn doll under the covers, the finger painting half-finished in the corner.

Can she hear me? "I'm so sorry."

Sun pours through the window with the pink curtains, strafing my face with unwanted morning. I sit up and carefully rearrange her blanket, making sure it's just the way she left it. Standing isn't an option. My feet are swollen and painful, and I'm certain there are some pieces of glass still embedded there.

I crawl out of her room and close the door, then return to my room. Pulling myself onto my bed, I lay on my side and fumble for the remote. The TV eventually clicks on, and Delilah's room comes into view. She's not there. Already gone to training.

Fuck.

Limping footsteps on my stairs tell me that Noah did, in fact, live through his beating.

"Adam?" He walks into my room, his gaze following the bloodied footprints.

"You look like hell." I squint at him—a black eye, busted lip, dried blood in his hair, and the aching sort of way he holds himself upright.

"No worse than you." He limps the rest of the way in and gingerly lowers himself to the mattress near my feet. "How did you manage this?" He peers at one foot.

"Minor household incident. You know." I pull open my nightstand and search around in the very back for my last pack of cigarettes. They're stale, no doubt, but necessary.

We light up, both of us pulling in a heavy drag, keeping it in and letting it burn before letting it out.

He stares at the orange tip of his cigarette for a moment, then says. "You were right."

"Yeah?" I take another pull.

"About your plan. About, you know, ending all this." He runs a hand through his hair, though his fingers get stuck at the spot with the matted blood. "You were right, and I was a pussy." He puts the cigarette between his lips, then thinks better of it. "I didn't know Dad would go that far. I thought..." He shrugs. "I don't know what I thought."

"Not a believer anymore?"

"Oh, I believe." He takes another drag. "I saw the fire before they beat the shit out of me."

I want to kick him, but my feet hurt too much. "Then what are we even talking about?"

He finally meets my gaze and lowers his voice to a whisper. "I believe that he speaks to the Father of Fire. That he is evil incarnate. And that you and I have to destroy him."

I would say amen if I were a religious sort. Instead, I just stare dumbfounded at him.

"Surprised?" He lets out a shaky laugh.

"To say the least." I finish my cigarette and stub it out, then wave at the ceiling fan. There's no way to know for sure that this place is bugged, but it's a good bet. "Later. We'll talk later."

He nods and lightens his tone. "I'll get the alcohol and try to fix your feet. They're pretty nasty, though." He sighs. "We've got to get you walking. He wants to see us this afternoon."

"Of course." I bottle my anger.

When he stands, I lean up and grab his arm. He looks at me, and something passes between us. He gives me a hard nod, and I let him go.

Whatever comes next, I'll have Noah at my back.

CHAPTER 17

DELILAH

I pull my knees up against me as Abigail does her usual muttering at the projector. No one has looked me in the eye this morning, and I'm glad. I can't deal with connection, or thoughts, or memories, or even feelings. Everything is cold, and every thought leads me back to Sarah. If I blink, I see Adam holding her in his arms. So I try to keep my eyes open, to keep the ugliness at bay. But it doesn't stop. It can't.

Grace walks in and hurries to the front of the room. She takes a moment, as if choosing her words, then begins, "I know that what happened last night may be shocking to some of you."

I would laugh if it wouldn't lead to a never-ending pit of sobs and grief.

She clasps her hands together in front of her and clears her throat. "But you have to understand that the Prophet knows God's plan. Sarah is blessed, sacred, and

133

holy. She will live forever in the light of our Lord, and the Prophet—"

"Killed her." Eve's voice, high and trembling, cuts through Grace's lies. "He made his son kill her. She isn't going to heaven. She's dead. Murdered. Right in front of all of us."

"Eve." Grace shakes her head. "That is the worldly interpretation of what happened, and is a blasphemy against the Prophet." She toys with the end of her baton. "Because I understand that emotions are running high, and because it is Christmas Day, I will let your comments pass. But if you tell any more lies, I'm afraid you won't escape punishment."

Eve covers her face with her hands and rocks back and forth.

"Good." Grace lets her gaze rove over the room. "As a Christmas treat, we will forego training for the day and, instead, will have a screening of 'The Passion of the Christ'."

I groan on the inside, but settle in for the movie. At least I won't have to interact with anyone. I've become an expert at blocking out whatever "instructional" video is playing and spending the time in my own head.

"Delilah." Grace's voice cracks over me like a whip. "Come with me."

My bones ache, and grief weighs me down, but I still can get no respite. Not even now. I stand and follow Grace from the room, her black skirt swishing against the cold wood floor. She leads me back to the dormitories and my room.

"Get dressed." She hands me a white dress that's similar to what I'm already wearing, but with a high collar and thicker fabric. "We're paying a visit to the Prophet's home."

"What? Why?"

She shoves me. I'm so weak that I stumble forward and fall onto the bed.

"Just do as you're told, Maiden!" She throws the dress at me. "Now!"

I strip my usual dress over my head as Grace watches. She inspects my nudity with a critical eye, as if she's adding up my shortcomings.

Once I'm dressed in the long gown and white flats, we leave my room. Chastity passes us in the hall, her hair up in a net and a vicious new bruise on her cheek.

Grace glances at me and smirks. "I saw her in your room. She broke the rules. She paid. The same way you will if you do anything to cross me on this little trip." She grabs my elbow and shoves me aside as she enters the code to open the outer door.

A golf cart waits just outside, one of the Protectors at the wheel. He tosses his half-smoked cigarette away. "Get in. It's fucking cold out here."

I sit on the back bench, and Grace settles in beside the driver, his greasy hair shining in the morning light. I stare at the road ahead as the cart moves smoothly up the pavement. Asking what this is about will get me nothing but a whack with Grace's baton. Does it have to do with Adam? I swallow hard as my mind falls into the next possible conclusion. Do they know the real reason I'm here? After what happened to Sarah, I have no illusions about what they'd do to me if they had any doubts about my loyalty to the Prophet. As far as they know, I broke in the Rectory and will never question the Prophet's divinity again. *Keep it that way.* I force myself to resume the mantle of brainwashed Maiden. Whatever happens, I have to play along, to convince the Prophet that I'm devout. It's no longer just about me infiltrating this place to find out about Georgia, now it's deeper, angrier, and more focused. I'll destroy them from the inside out.

We roll to a stop at the rear of the huge Georgian mansion, and the Protector walks up to a set of back doors. After entering a code, he opens the nearest door and ushers us inside.

I follow Grace, matching my footsteps to hers as we pass a bar, a pool table, some chairs, and corridors on either side that lead deeper into the lower levels of the basement. One door to my right has what looks like a metal plank that can be thrown to bar it.

We climb a staircase that opens into a luxurious foyer. Everything here gleams—the wood, the marble floors, even the artwork. It takes a moment for my eyes to adjust, and I realize just how austere and oddly woodsy the Cloister is in comparison.

"In here." Grace points to a sitting room with a piano in one corner, a large fireplace, and various couches and chairs. "Sit down, don't touch anything, and don't speak to anyone until I come back." She delivers her edict with narrowed eyes before disappearing farther into the foyer.

I sit on the end of a leather sofa and stare at the fine

things the Prophet can afford from all the tithes he collects in the Lord's name. Just one piece of furniture or art in this room could have funded quite a few semesters for me at Alabama. I run my fingers down the buttery soft leather. The house even smells rich—like some sort of sweet cigar scent mixed with furniture polish and money.

Faint voices barely make it to my ear, but I can't tell what they're saying or where they are. I shrink back into the cushions and focus on the steady thump of my heart. It still beats, despite what it's been through, despite what I've seen, despite the pain of losing Georgia and Sarah. How it manages to keep going, I'll never know. What's worse, is that it's a traitor. Even now, I peer out into the foyer and hope for a glimpse of Adam. He murdered my friend before my eyes only a few hours ago, but I still seek him out. It's wrong, and I hate myself for it, but my heart—that bruised and battered organ—still yearns for him. I shake my head at myself.

A door clicks open nearby, and then footsteps approach. I fold my hands in my lap and stare at the floor —the picture of perfect obedience.

"Delilah." The Prophet's voice stabs into the room.

I stand but keep my gaze downcast. "Yes, Prophet." Clenching my eyes shut, I wait for some sort of accusation from him, maybe even a sentence, since he's judge, jury, and executioner on the compound.

"Good girl." He comes in and stands in front of me, his shoes gleaming along with everything else. "I have a visitor to see you."

That's it? "Yes, Prophet." I keep the relief out of my voice, even though it washes over me like a tidal wave.

"Treat him nicely, and give him the blessing of your holy presence." He lowers his voice. "But nothing more."

How different he is than his son. Adam hates it when I don't look him in the eye. The Prophet prefers it.

"I understand, Prophet."

"Good girl."

I wonder if he'll pat my head like a dog. But he doesn't, simply strides away.

His shoes are replaced by another set, this pair not quite as shiny, and the door to the foyer closes.

"Delilah." Evan reaches out to take my hand and smiles down at me.

"What are you doing here?"

He sits on the couch and pulls me down next to him. "I simply couldn't wait."

"For what?" I meet his gaze. The Prophet isn't here to see my little rebellion.

He wraps an arm around my shoulder. "To put in a bid."

Hatred, the sort that eats away at you like a poison, saturates my blood. "Oh?"

"I want you, Delilah. For myself." He runs his fingers down my cheek. "All of you. Not the Prophet's leftovers."

I want to bite his fingers off. Instead, I remain still and let him talk.

"I'll have to marry you—that's one of the Prophet's rules that can't be broken, but I don't mind. A woman like you would make the perfect wife. Obedient, mostly." He grins knowingly. "But I know there's a little bite back inside you, and that's one of the reasons I want you. I'll get to break you myself." He grabs a strand of my white hair and rubs it between his fingers. "And you're perfect for breeding."

"Get off." I slap his hand away.

"There it is." He grabs my wrist and squeezes it until my eyes water. "That little something extra. You know, I've been coming here for years, checking out the crops of little virgins the Prophet collects. But you're the first one that's caught my eye." He reaches for my throat with his free hand.

I scoot back, but he yanks me forward by my wrist, then slams me back onto the couch. When I cry out, I expect the Prophet or maybe Grace to barge through the door. No one comes.

"Stop!" I struggle as he yanks at the button closure at my throat, then rips my dress open. "Grace!" Desperation puts her name on my tongue.

"No one's coming." He grabs a handful of my hair and holds me in place while he rips my dress the rest of the way off. "But don't worry, I'll play by the rules." He sits back and stares at me, his gaze roving over my nudity.

Hot tears pool in my eyes, and I struggle to free myself. He only pulls my hair harder and keeps me pinned to the leather.

"I'm going to let you go." He pulls a phone from his pocket. "And take some pics. But if you fight me, I'll hurt you." He whips a hand back and hurtles it toward my face, halting only an inch away. "Next time, I won't stop. Don't fucking move."

Tears inch down my temples as he releases me and stands back. With one hand, he pushes my knee aside, opening me to him. He licks his lips, and I close my eyes to try and go to some other place. A place where this isn't happening.

"Open your eyes. I want to see the tears."

I shake my head, but do as he says.

"That's it."

I can't hear the click of the camera, but he stands still every so often. He takes a close up between my legs and violates me every way possible without actually touching me.

"Now I want you to say 'please stop, Evan'." He stands over me, the bulge in his pants impossible to miss. "Say it like you mean it."

"Please stop, Evan." I do mean it.

He moves the phone closer to my face, as if he's focusing on my tears. "Beg me to stop."

"Please stop." I speak to him, not the camera, but he is looking at me through a lens and nothing more.

"Ask me not to hurt you." He runs the heel of his palm across his hard cock.

Humiliation overwhelms every other emotion firing inside my head. It's all too much.

He grabs my hair and grates at me, "I said 'ask me not to hurt you.'"

I don't feel myself snap so much as I simply act. My

left hand curls into a fist, and I jab it straight out, nailing him in the crotch.

He lets out a yelp and falls to his knees.

I jump up from the couch and run to the door. Though I twist it and yank the handle as hard as I can, it doesn't move. A primal scream tears from my lungs as I beat on the door.

A groan from behind me—too close behind me— makes me turn around. Evan's face is bright red, his eyes lit with fury, as he rushes toward me with one hand on his crotch.

I scream and dart to the side, then wedge myself behind the piano.

He lurches around to me, then leans on the keys with a discordant noise and takes a deep breath. "Bitch."

"Fuck you." I'll fight and claw and scream and kick and do whatever the hell I have to do to keep him from touching me ever again. "Come near me again, and I'll go for your fucking eyes." My voice is a hiss, the promise of violence despite the odds. He's too big, too strong, and I know I'll lose, but I'll take a piece of him with me if it's the last thing I do.

The door bursts open, and Grace and the Prophet rush in.

Grace stops, her mouth agape, and the Prophet points at me and shouts, "You goddamn harlot! Get out from behind there!"

I don't move.

He steps closer, the kindly man mask falling away

and replaced with hateful indignation. "Girl, you do as I say!"

"Delilah!" Grace's voice is shrill as she edges around the other side of the piano, trying to cut me off. "You're ruining your placement, disappointing the Prophet, and forgetting your place."

Evan holds a hand out behind him, but doesn't take his eyes off me. "It's fine."

"Fine?" Grace turns to him, her eyebrows high.

He smiles and straightens. "This is what I want. *Exactly* what I want. When can I have her?"

CHAPTER 18

ADAM

*N*oah helps me to my chair, then sinks into his with a sigh. We're both beat up, but we're stronger now than we've ever been. United.

My father sits at his desk, perusing us with his cunning gaze.

Castro sits off to the side, an assault rifle casually balanced across his thighs.

"Now that the solstice is over, we have a lot to discuss." My father leans back in his chair and continues on as if we hadn't just murdered an innocent girl, "The first phase of Monroeville is well on its way to completion. But there are other areas that need improvement. The land to the southwest needs to be completely cleared and the fields readied for planting this spring. Noah, I'm assigning that acreage to you."

"Me?" Noah cocks his head. "No disrespect, Dad, but I don't know a thing about farming."

He waves a dismissive hand. "You don't have to. The

Father of Fire will provide. We're in his good graces. Get the Caldwells from the hardware shop on board. They'll help you get started with equipment and know-how. And Zion's family owns a farm down near Andalusia. He'll be your second-in-command."

"Zion?" Noah is incredulous. "The same Zion who did this?" He points to his black eye and the blood crusting in his hair.

"That's behind us. We all played the parts we had to. The Lord has forgiven Zion and so should you." He turns to me. "You proved yourself last night. It took a little arm twisting, but you did what needed to be done."

I don't know if he expects me to thank him for forcing me to kill Sarah, but I'll be damned if those words ever cross my lips.

He sighs. "Now that you've finally come into the fold, I'd like you to take a bigger role in running the Cloister. Grace has been adequate, and we'll still continue to use her, but leaving a woman in charge of anything of importance is never a good idea. Women aren't meant for leadership, her included."

I cross one leg over the other and hide my wince as the wounds on my feet burn and ache. "What would you have me do?"

"The suitors. I've already been dealing with an over-eager one." A sly smile twists his lips. "You may remember him, Evan Roberts, the senator."

Of course I remember that piece of shit. I shrug. "I can't keep up with everyone who comes and goes."

"He was already here this morning, wanting to try on your Maiden for size."

Everything in me tightens, as if I'm being pulled taut over a rack. "Oh?"

"Yes." His smile turns into a smirk. "Took some detailed photos of her. Very in-depth. I saved a set for myself. Oh, and the video—the things he made her say while she cried—priceless."

My nails dig into the arms of the leather chair, but I force myself to relax. He's intentionally turning the screws, but I won't let him see how much hate he unleashes with each twist. "Is he ready to pay up?"

My father shrugs. "He didn't come to negotiate, so his eagerness is going to cost him. I put double the usual price on her, and he accepted without complaint. It'll take him a week or so to scrape together the funds from offshore accounts and campaign funds, but he'll get it. I've never seen a man so hungry for a Maiden before. It's perfect, really. I've asked Miriam to come and give her one-on-one classes about extracting information, knowing what's relevant, and getting that information back to me. She'll be leading the senator around by his dick in no time."

"What does any of this have to do with me?" I keep my tone unconcerned, even though I'm burning for every fucking detail he has to offer.

"First, you are not to leave any more marks on her. That was one of his requests that I think we can meet. He also asked that she not be touched at all until he comes to claim her."

I still. "I'm expected to follow that request too?"

"No." He opens his drawer to retrieve a joint. His book sits on the edge of the desk, the black leather cover hiding the tangle of insanity within the pages. He only takes it out around the winter and summer solstices, keeping it hidden away for the rest of the year. "She's not bought and paid for, so as far as I'm concerned, you can carry on. But, no marks. He doesn't want her marred."

Acid pushes up my throat. I swallow hard. "Are you going to claim her before she goes?"

"That's another one of his requests. A demand, really. He wants her pure or no deal." He drops the book into a lower drawer and locks it. "I have to be honest." He meets my eye again. "I've wanted to fuck her since the moment I saw her in the congregation. That weird white hair and skin get me hard every time."

Don't make a move. After what I did last night, strangling him with my bare hands seems easy.

"But." He shrugs. "I'm going to let him have her virgin pussy. After all, he's a senator, the most powerful client we've had yet. Getting a Maiden in his ear is far more valuable than some bitch's twat, even if it's the prettiest shade of pink I've ever seen." He leers at me. "Hell, I was kind of hoping no one would claim her and she'd go to the Cathedral. Breeding her would be interesting. Maybe our kids would have that fairy shit going for them too."

Even though his words are like razors cutting through the flesh of my ears, for once I'm glad that my father likes to hear himself talk. I'll take whatever information he wants to give. Especially if he's telling me that Delilah will be safe—at least for a week until she's delivered to the senator.

"When's the wedding?" Noah asks.

"A month."

Part of the contract on the Maidens is that the claiming suitor *must* marry them. Otherwise, the Prophet wouldn't get a real foothold. The suitor could toss them aside and move on to his next conquest. The main way to get the suitors to stick to the deal is to withhold the Maiden until the day of the wedding so that he's desperate to fuck her, and happy to say "I do." "You expect him to keep his dick out of her for a month? She should stay here."

"I can bend the rules for him. Doesn't matter to me if he fucks her every which way he pleases, as long as he shows up on the wedding day. I've already got plenty of video from his visit this morning that he definitely wouldn't want getting to the press. So I'm not worried about his commitment." He pulls out his coke box. "Aside from that, I have another set of suitors in line for most of the other girls. Seems like everyone is jumping the gun this year. I want you to speak with them, cool them off, tell them the Maidens need the year of training in order to be perfect helpmates. We can't go selling them all off before I've had a chance to make sure they're loyal. Not to mention I need some of them for the Chapel and the Cathedral. And I've been thinking, we're going to lower the age limit for the Cloister to 16." His eyes flash with greed. "We'll get purer girls that way, easier to train, not stained by the outside world. We'll get waivers from their parents, no problem." He pauses and rubs his chin. "Maybe we should say 14 instead of 16. The purest virgin bodies."

I swallow my disgust and change the subject. "So I'm supposed to babysit hard-up suitors and take over the Cloister on top of handling the contracts for Monroeville, collecting the cash from the dealers in Birmingham, and keeping our books clean for the IRS? Anything else you need me to do?"

He arranges a neat line of powder and gives me a harsh grin. "Oh, I think you did plenty last night."

My guts churn. The hatred must show on my face because Castro taps the butt of his gun and gives me a withering look.

I stand, forcing my throbbing feet to bear my weight.

"But I do have one more little task for you." He frowns as Noah struggles to rise, his body probably aching worse than mine. "That apostate we kicked out, the one you beat the shit out of a month or so ago, what was his name?"

"Drew," Castro offers. "Something like that."

A memory flutters and lands. "Davis? Chris Davis, the former lieutenant?"

"That's the one." My father shoots an imaginary pistol at me with his fingers. "He's been snooping around the edges of the compound ever since we kicked him out. Doesn't seem like he got the message the first time. Find him and make sure he gets it this go-around."

I can barely stand, yet my father expects me to go

MMA on Davis. Fuck, maybe I can just shoot the guy and call it a day.

"Out. I've got visitors coming. The mayor of Birmingham doesn't need to see you two sorry sacks of shit, especially not for a Christmas tea." He turns his attention to his coke habit as we limp into the foyer and down to the basement. I can feel blood oozing from my left foot, the one that took the brunt of the "safety" glass when I walked through it last night.

I dig the heels of my palms into my eyes to try and grind away the images that I know will haunt me for the rest of my life, however short that may be. But Sarah is still there, her drugged eyes wide, her blood spilling in a warm crimson rush.

"What should we do first?" Noah grabs a bottle from the dwindling supply behind the bar.

I force myself back to the here and now. "Well, Old MacDonald, I guess you need to get your ass over to the farmland and see how much work it'll take to clear all that acreage."

He groans and twists the cap off, letting it fall onto the wood floor and roll away. "Fuck that. I'd rather help you with Davis."

"How can you help?" I poke him in the ribs.

He doubles over. "Motherfucker!"

"Those are cracked, you're probably pissing blood, and let's not even talk about the limp." I take the bottle from him and swallow two huge gulps. The burn is getting easier, and I can see how Noah has fallen into the alcohol, drugging himself as best he can.

"I can drive."

"I'll get an address." We'll pay Davis a visit at his home. See if he wants to keep shitting where he eats. "But we're going to have to play this one smart. My feet are fucked, the rest of you is fucked, and we can't give him the idea that we're weak."

"I'm working on numbing it all." He takes another big swig.

I snatch the bottle from him and smash it on the floor. "Don't kill yourself just yet. We've got too much shit to do, and I'm not talking about our Prophet-assigned tasks."

He wipes his mouth with his sleeve and nods, but casts a mournful glance at the wasted liquor. "Right. You're right. I've got to get it together... One question."

"Yeah?"

"Can we do it tomorrow?" He wraps an arm around his midsection. "I think I need to lie down."

I shake my head but relent. "Sure, I guess. He didn't give us a time limit."

"Thank you." He leans on the bar, all the bravado gone.

"I'll get you back to your place."

"You not coming?"

"Nah." I hobble to the back door. "It's almost time for me to see Delilah."

He whistles and limps out behind me. "You think she wants to see you?"

"No." I shrug. "But she's going to."

CHAPTER 19

DELILAH

*M*y bedroom door opens. I know it's him. I could feel him coming down the hall, even though his footsteps are off somehow.

I don't get up, just lie with my back to him, the blanket drawn up to my shoulder. Grace reamed me the entire way back to the Cloister after my "reckless assault" on the senator. But at least she didn't lay a hand on me, no matter how badly she'd wanted to.

Exhausted in every way that counts, I'd returned to my room and got into my bed. Haven't moved since.

"Delilah." His quiet voice crosses the barren landscape of distance between us.

I don't look at him, because if I do, I'll cry. The tears are already there, waiting to be shed. For Sarah, for me, even for him.

Some shuffling noises, and then the bed shifts—he slips under the blanket behind me and wraps his arms around me. I don't struggle or protest when he pulls my back against his warm chest and nuzzles into my hair. There's a gentleness to his touch. He isn't taking. Not this time.

I sigh and relax a little, breathing him in. He must have just showered because he smells like soap along with some sort of faint antiseptic scent. Rubbing alcohol?

"Are you hurt?" The question escapes before I can stop it.

"No. Are you?"

I turn over, my dress twisting around my torso, and look into his eyes. As I predicted, mine start to water.

"Are you hurt?" he asks again.

"Yes." My word breaks on a sob, and he pulls me tight to him, my hot tears rolling down his neck and bare chest as he rubs my back. The same hands he used to take Sarah's life, and I can't reconcile the two. I'll never be able to. But I can't stop the river of emotion that pours out of me, and I don't want to leave the safety of his arms. It's false—I know it is. His strength isn't real, not when he can be so easily crushed by the Prophet. But right now, here in this room, it's enough for me.

"Shh, it's okay." His voice is gravelly, as if his anguish mirrors my own.

I don't know how long I cry. Long minutes of hot tears and anger and sorrow run together until I'm finally spent, every last bit of grief wrung from me like bloody water from a washcloth. He still rubs my back and shushes me softly.

I wipe my face on the sleeve of my dress and pull back enough to look at him. He blinks several times and runs a hand over his face. But I don't miss the wetness on his lashes. My heart would break for him if it wasn't already dusted and scattered to the four winds.

"I didn't want to. I swear to you." He strokes my cheek. "I've killed before. Plenty of times. I'm not a good man. But I swear on—" He blinks hard, his eyes watering, and his voice lowers to a barely audible whisper. "On my daughter's grave that I did not want to kill your friend."

I've never seen a person in so much pain, the anguish spilling over and coloring everything in shades of gloomy gray and funeral black. I catch a single tear that rolls from his eye and wonder at it, at the man who seemed made of stone that now lies crumbled before me.

"You had a daughter?"

He nods, but doesn't speak, as if saying more might cause injury. I recognize the bitter taste of mourning, the same unyielding pain I felt when Georgia died, but perhaps even deeper since he lost a child.

"I'm sorry."

"Me too." He holds me so close I can feel the steady thump of his heart against my chest.

There's nothing else to say. Not really. I want to know more, but I don't want to probe a wound that still bleeds. He gives me the same courtesy, not mentioning another word about Sarah.

He hasn't said that he didn't kill Georgia. I haven't asked. And I won't, because I already know the answer. The misery consuming him at this moment is truth enough. Sarah is the first innocent he's sacrificed. I wish I could tell him that I'm here to make sure it never happens again. To end this place for Georgia ... and maybe even for us. But some secrets are best left unspoken.

Instead, I say, "Someone bought me." The words should strike me as absurd, but they don't. Evan Roberts is all too real, his threat palpable.

"I know."

"Don't let him take me." God, I sound weak, and I hate it.

"I'm going to do whatever I can to keep you away from him."

"Like what?"

He doesn't hold back, giving me a frank gaze and the truth. "I don't know yet, but I'm working on getting us out."

"I punched him in the dick," I blurt.

He smiles. Jesus Christ and all the angels, he's actually smiling, and I can't believe how much I long to see more of it. Pure and warm—nothing like the darkness that usually envelops him.

"Your eyes got so big right then." He streaks his fingertips along my temple.

"I've just never seen you... happy."

"Tell you what. You keep dick-punching that motherfucker, and I'll keep being happy."

I smile and press my lips to his. "Deal," I whisper against him.

He doesn't need more of an invitation. He grabs a handful of my ass and yanks me against him as his tongue wars and wins against mine. His embrace is warm, and delicious, and wrong in so many ways, but I crave it all the same. Throwing one leg around his hips, I scoot closer. He surges forward, his cock pressing against me, the only things separating us a few layers of inconsequential fabric.

After a while, he shifts away from me, and I find myself panting, wanting more of his kiss.

He squeezes my ass again. "I have to hurt you. For the camera."

"Oh." I press my open palm against his chest. "You don't like hurting me anymore?"

"I love it." He snakes a hand up my stomach and grips one breast, kneading it roughly. "But only on my terms. Not for anyone else. Just us."

"Us?"

He covers my hand with his. "Us."

We're both raw, trapped animals, forced to perform for the crowd night after night.

"Let's do this for us, then." I kick off the blanket, then rise onto my knees and strip my dress over my head.

He tenses and scores my body with his gaze. My already-hard nipples start to ache as he stares at them. Something dangerous lights his eyes, and a shiver courses through me.

"All fours," he grates.

I prowl down to the bed and watch him.

"Oh, little lamb, you know what I like." He lifts himself onto his knees beside me and presses my face and chest to the bed with a steady hand on my upper back. He smooths his other palm over my ass in slow circles. "I can't leave a mark on you."

I can only breathe into the mattress as his circles grow smaller and smaller until his fingers dip between my legs and stroke my wet folds. His touch sends sparks of tension swirling inside me, the threads holding me together pulling tighter and tighter.

"But what I give you right now will fade." He rears back and brings his hand rushing forward with a loud slap, a rush of pain following behind like thunder after the lightning.

I grip the sheet and try to take a breath, but the blows come hard and fast, each one sending stinging pain through my skin and a jolt up my spine. God, it hurts, and I'm almost to the point of trying to stop him when he dips his fingers between my thighs again, pulsing them against my slick core and moving quickly.

I moan, and he speeds up, his touch verging on too rough and not enough. I rock my hips, searching for the one electric road leading to my release.

"Not so fast, little lamb." His fingers retreat, and his hand comes down on my ass again, slap after stinging slap.

"Adam!" I push against the hand holding me down, but he doesn't let up.

More pain and then his fingers snake between my thighs again, demanding my compliance. I give it, grinding myself against his fingers as the cocktail of pleasure and pain shoots through my bloodstream, taking me to a new high. Right there, on the edge of release, I tense, so close to that perfect explosion.

He takes his fingers away. I scream into the mattress

and buck when his hand comes down hard again. He doesn't show any mercy, only hits me until I'm a quivering heap, everything inside me drawn relentlessly tense. When his fingers press against the hot, needy flesh at my core, I moan low and long.

"Now, little lamb." He strokes me in hard, consistent movements.

It doesn't take long until my body freezes, then bursts outward in an electric blast of release. I cry and writhe, the pleasure more than I've ever felt, almost too much for me to bear. When the waves finally crest and fall back into the deep well of the ocean, I go limp, my body too shaky to do anything other than lie down.

He rubs my ass with both hands, soothing the ache. I can't think, only feel. And I feel everything—his hands, my throbbing clit, the rough sheets beneath me, the need for him that eclipses everything else.

When he drops a kiss on my back, I tremble and turn to him. I need his arms around me, his secrets whispered in my ear. But he backs off the bed, wincing when his feet touch the floor.

"What is it?" Using the last of my strength, I roll to his side of the bed. "What's wrong with your feet?"

"Nothing." He pulls on his button-up and straightens the collar. "Stepped on some glass is all."

"Glass?" My brain can't connect any dots. Not right now. "Does it hurt?"

He shrugs. "A little, but it'll heal."

I want to tell him I'm sorry, that I wish I could fix it—but those are things that can only be whispered in his ear.

Not out loud so the Prophet or Grace or whoever can use it against him, can use *me* against him. I graze the small line on my neck where the Protector cut me while Adam... No, I won't think of what Adam was doing that night at the bonfire. I can't.

"Goodnight, little lamb." He doesn't kiss me, though I can feel how much he wants to from the heated look in his eye. Turning away, he walks to the door with uncertain, pained steps. "Merry Christmas," he whispers as he closes the door.

CHAPTER 20

ADAM

*D*elilah haunts my nightmares, her gray eyes pleading with me as my father carves runes into her flesh with a rusty blade. Protectors hold me back, forcing me to my knees as Noah takes the curved knife, readying it to cut Delilah's life away in steady strokes.

I wake in a sweat. The TV screen gives the only light in the room, and I turn to watch her sleeping. She's kicked her sheet off, her dress tangled at her hips as she lies on her stomach. I can't see her face, but I know she's beautiful. A pleasant dream, one free from the terrors of the Cloister—that's what I wish for her as I watch the slow rise and fall of her breathing.

It soothes me to know she's beyond the clutches of my father. Safe in slumber, at least for now. I shift onto my back, and pain ricochets up my legs. But I can bear it. That's the trick—bearing it. Whatever my father throws at me, I can bear it. And I'll keep on bearing it until it's time for me to take him down. All I need is a window, and I'm determined to take it the second I see it.

I doze in and out for a few more hours, just catching sight of Delilah is enough to soothe me to sleep in steady swaths. When the sun finally rears its head, I watch as she rises and readies for the morning. She casts a glance at the camera before leaving her room for training. Does she know I'm watching?

Hauling myself out of bed takes some work, but I shamble to the bathroom, using a cleared path through the glass, and turn on the tub faucet. It takes a while to undo Noah's wraps on my feet, but once they're clear, I sink into the warm water. The sting reminds me I'm alive, and I get to work washing myself.

Noah's stumping up my stairs by the time I'm out and toweling off.

The bruises on his face have darkened even more, the first step to healing.

He eyes my feet. "I brought more alcohol and bandages from my place."

"They'll be fine." I finger comb my hair.

"Shut up." He walks in. "Sit on the counter and try to keep your junk out of my face."

I turn and slide onto the vanity. "Not my fault it's so big."

He laughs a little, and I realize how long it's been since we've done this—actually behaved like brothers instead of two cogs in a crushing machine.

"Shit!" I hiss when he douses the soles of my feet

with alcohol. "Your bedside manner could use a little work."

"Stop crying." He inspects the cuts. "They aren't super bad, but if they get infected, you'll regret it." After wrapping my feet in gauze, he stands and winces.

"You going to make it?"

"Yeah. Just sore." He finger combs his own damp hair in my mirror—a younger, lighter version of myself. God, what potential he had. He could be a family man, a lawyer; hell, even a garbage man is better than what we do here. I turn away and hobble to my closet instead of dwelling on all we've lost.

Once I've dressed, we limp down the stairs, and I let out a gallows laugh at what a mess we are.

"You packing?" I already tucked my usual Glock into my shoulder holster.

"Yep." He opens the front door and a gust of wintery wind blows inside.

"Good." I grab my black coat from the hall and follow him out. "We're too fucking sorry to do it with our fists. Metal will have to suffice."

We ride out to the front gate, numerous cars already parked around the sanctuary for the annual day-after-Christmas yard sale. Rows of tables have been lined up along the western side of the church, and members stack items for sale. All proceeds are supposed to go to the "Heavenly Missionaries Fund," but the Prophet will pocket what little money the churchgoers make from selling last year's toys, dusty knick-knacks, or whatever Christmas gifts they don't want.

Everything Heavenly does is one hustle or another, but at this point, I wonder if the members would even care if they knew the truth. They already tithe ridiculous amounts to the Prophet. What's a little more?

"Hmph." Noah turns onto the highway that runs along one edge of the compound.

"What?"

"Nothing. Just saw a skateboard on a table back there that reminded me of..." He shrugs and lets the memory fade into the ether.

"I probably still have the moves, you know. Could do some sick tricks."

He chuckles. "You didn't have the moves when we were kids. There's no way you've got them now."

I rub my chin. There isn't a scar from where I kissed the curb so long ago, but I don't need raised skin to remind me of what was stripped away from us that day.

"Which way?" He slows as we approach the interstate that circles the southern half of Birmingham.

"North. He lives in that new development on the upper Cahaba."

"Got it." He flicks on the radio and turns it up.

"So, is there a plan?"

I can barely hear him over the music. He's smart to suspect the car's bugged.

I nod.

"What is it?"

"We have to do it during the Tuesday night ceremony. When he's preoccupied with the Maidens at the Temple."

He glances at me, his forehead wrinkled. "But he's surrounded by Protectors."

"I didn't promise an easy plan. Just a plan." It could be suicide, but with Delilah's future on the line, I have to move fast. She's supposed to be sold on Wednesday. So it's Tuesday or not at all.

"Shit." He passes several cars on the right, the speedometer needle hovering at 100. Not that it matters. No one around here would dare pull over a black Mercedes with a Heavenly tag.

"What about Mom?"

Every plan has kinks. "As soon as we're done at the Temple, we'll have to head to the house and surprise Castro and his team of fuckwads. We'll get the drop on them and take them out before they even get her door unlocked."

"How? One of the Protectors will surely warn them about what's going down. There's no way this can work." He shakes his head.

"The Protectors can't warn anyone if they're dead, Noah." I shoot him a smirk.

He pales a little and swallows hard. "So... so you're saying we—"

"Kill them all." There's no other way to ensure Heavenly crumbles. "If we don't destroy the power players, one of them will rise up and become the new Prophet. That means every Protector has to go down."

"All of them." He seems to be saying it more to himself than to me.

I respond anyway, "Every last one of those sons-of-bitches."

"Right." He nods a little too forcefully. "Right. That's the way it has to be."

Killing isn't in his blood, not the way it's in mine. But he's going to have to get his hands dirty if we want to get out of this alive. Leaving even one snake alive would mean we'd have to be on alert for the rest of our lives. No. They all have to go.

He turns the music down and takes a right onto the exit for Cahaba Estates.

I switch gears smoothly. "We're going to play it cool until we get in the door. I'll take the lead from there on out. Just remember, keep your pistol handy since we're fucked otherwise."

"I got it." He slows as the GPS leads us around a sharp curve and then into a new neighborhood with only ten of about fifty home-sites completed. "It's this one." He stops in front of a white Craftsman-style house with a nice front porch and brand new landscaping.

"Pretty nice digs for a guy who just got the boot from Heavenly." I climb out of the car and use all my effort to keep my walk steady and normal despite the pain. "Did he already get another job?"

"Nope." Noah joins me on the short sidewalk. "Dad blacklisted him. No law enforcement office in the state will hire him."

I eye the side windows next to the door and point for Noah to wait out of sight beside them. He gets in position and gives me a sharp nod, his gun hand inside his coat.

After glancing around and seeing no neighbors or cars, I knock.

Shuffling sounds, and then the door opens a crack.

I immediately throw my weight against it, knocking Davis onto his ass at the foot of a staircase. Noah and I rush in and slam the door behind us. Davis yells and scrambles to sit up.

"He's reaching!" Noah shouts as I dive onto the asshole and wrestle his arms out to his sides. He's got a sleek black pistol in his right hand. I slam his wrist onto the wood floor twice, and the second vicious impact sends the piece skittering away.

"Stop!" He struggles.

I cock my fist back. Maybe I won't need to use my gun after all.

Then he says something that freezes my fist and my blood.

"Stop, FBI!"

CHAPTER 21

*A*bigail pats the enema table and waves me over. "Glad to see you back in training."

That makes one of us. I climb up and assume the position as Mary, the most devout Maiden, takes the table next to me.

Abigail futzes about with the water while the other Maidens form a ring around the teaching Spinner.

"Today, we're going to address the subject of strap-ons," she announces, her face reddening.

I let my head hang between my shoulders, ready to block out whatever the Spinner says next.

"Delilah." Mary leans toward me.

"Yeah?" I turn my head in her direction.

"What was the Rectory like?"

"Why? You intend to go there?"

Abigail spreads my cheeks, and I clench my teeth.

"No, of course not." She frowns. "I just wanted to know, is all."

"Curiosity will get you sent there, so I'd mind my business if I were you." I suppose she thinks I've forgotten about how she prevented Sharon's short-lived bid for escape. Not a chance. I look for the strawberry blonde in the crowd. She's along the back row, her head down, her hands clasped in front of her, her ribs protruding. Sharon's time in the Rectory ended before mine, but the results are the same.

"I just wanted to—"

Abigail smacks her ass, and Mary yelps. "No talking on my watch. No ma'am."

I take a little satisfaction in Abigail's uncharacteristically rough treatment of Mary. Maybe she remembers Sharon's escape attempt, too. I can't be entirely sure about Abigail. Is she devoted to the Prophet? I have no doubt of it. Does she like the way the Cloister operates? I think she has misgivings, at the very least.

She could be useful, but I've never gotten her to open up more than the day when Grace broke my finger. I still wonder what she meant by Grace visiting someone at night. Who?

When she pats my lower back and says "release," I let go of the warm water, and she cleans me up, then shoos me over to the training session. Eve is on all fours, her eyes clenched shut, and Susannah is on her knees behind her, a purple dildo strapped to her with black leather.

"Do not penetrate her maidenhood," the Spinner warns, then guides Susannah forward until the shiny purple tip presses against Eve's asshole. "This is a skill that plenty of men will appreciate. Many like to give and receive, and with a strap-on device, you can bring him ultimate pleasure. Of course, the female anatomy is different, and lacks the prostate, which is what you will be aiming for whenever you perform this act." She walks over and grabs a small bottle of lube from the implements wall, then hands it to Susannah. "You'll need to lubricate every time."

She spreads the lube and follows the Spinner's instructions, pushing halfway inside as Eve's tears plop onto the mat beneath her. I wish I could help her, could make this needless torture end. But I can't. Not yet.

And the worst part is—the humiliation doesn't even faze me anymore.

After a lunch where I spend far too much time staring at Sarah's empty seat, Grace pulls me from class and orders me to dress in the same high-necked gown from my last visit to the Prophet's house. My stomach is queasy, my food turning to acid as I follow her out the back door and onto the same golf cart that takes us up to the house. We walk into the warm basement, and I already hate the familiar scent of the house.

"If you pull another stunt like you did last time, it won't matter what your suitor wants, I *will* punish you." Grace grabs my chin and yanks my face to hers as the back door closes. "Are we clear?"

"Clear."

"Good." She releases me and leads me up to the main floor and back to the same sitting room as before.

I sit in a different spot, but it doesn't stop my heart from raging in my chest, my blood pounding, and my breaths coming in quick bursts.

"Get it together." I wipe my sweaty palms on my dress and peer around the room. Maybe there's something in here I can use. A weapon? That wouldn't end well, given Grace's threat, but I don't care. I won't let him use me like he did the last time.

Footsteps in the hall raise my hackles, but I let out a breath of relief when Adam strides in, his walk a little off.

"What is it?" I stand and take a step toward him, but he shakes his head at me ever-so-slightly, his eyes hard.

I return to my seat and lace my fingers together.

"I'll be overseeing your joining with Evan." His voice is cold, and I know it's an act, but it doesn't stop a chill from racing down my spine.

"My joining?"

He lets out a bored sigh. "You never seem to have a hearing problem during our sessions at the Cloister."

"Ass," I hiss.

He smirks but continues, "Evan is to be treated with respect at all times. He's your future husband..." He pauses at that, the mask cracking, but gets it together. "You are expected to please him in every way. His word is law. The only person he answers to is the Prophet. You will follow your husband's word to the letter and be in perfect obedience. If you fail to do so, there will be punishment."

I glare at him and cross my arms over my stomach.

He moves closer, but doesn't touch me. When I reach out, he steps back and glances at the ceiling fan, then gives me a pointed look.

Right, cameras.

"I won't tell you these rules again. If you break them, be assured that Evan is well within his rights to dole out your punishment as he sees fit. Perfect obedience is the only way for you to remain in his good graces. Do you understand?"

I nod.

He approaches and tilts my chin up, his touch gentle even as he barks, "I asked you if you understood."

I jump. "Yes!"

I catch the scent of his soap and the unease in his eyes. His broad back blocks the camera, and I turn my head and kiss his palm. The ghost of a smile graces his lips, and he slides his fingertips along my jaw, softly stroking my cheek before letting his hand fall back to his side. "Good."

Without another word, he turns on his heel and strides out. Low voices in the hall reverberate into the sitting room, and I settle deeper into the sofa, looking for any sort of defense the furniture can provide.

When Evan walks in, I sink farther, hoping for invisibility that I know won't come.

"Don't be like that, darling." He smiles broadly and sits next to me.

Too close, he slings his arm around my shoulders.

My ears go hot, my hands cold, and I can't seem to catch my breath.

"I have that effect on women." He pulls me into his lap, his arms locking me in place.

I can't escape. My heart is trying to claw its way from my chest.

"Shhh, calm down. I'm not going to hurt you. All that from yesterday is done." He squeezes me. "I promise."

Breathe, breathe, breathe.

"And I'll even forgive and forget about that little move you pulled on me, okay? We can start fresh." His easy southern drawl and All-American good looks don't fool me. He's a demon underneath, one that wants to eat me alive. "Shhh, now. Everything's going to be just fine."

I force myself to relax, to just *be*, even though he's got me trapped. Untethering is the only way. I close my eyes and go somewhere else—Georgia's room at her parent's house. Warm sun, a fluffy comforter, and notebooks with her drawings and my writing spread out all around us.

"Do you think I could, I don't know, draw for a living?" She has a swipe of blue ink on her cheek, but I don't mention it.

"I think you can do anything you want to do."

She laughs, mistaking my earnestness for sarcasm. "Well, I think you can, too. What do you want to do, anyway? You decided on a major yet?"

I twirl my pencil. "Yeah, I think I want to be in law enforcement."

She gawks. "A cop?"

"No." I shake my head. "More like CSI. I like figuring things out, you know?"

"Makes sense." She adds a dash of pink to one of her drawings—it's of a dress with fantastic lace and ribbon, too girly to be true. "You've always been good at solving mysteries."

"Darling." He tucks my hair behind my ear. "What's wrong?"

I shake my head and pull myself back to the present. "What do you want?"

"Straight to the point, aren't you?" He smooths one hand down my thigh.

I pinch my lips together.

"Not going to talk today?" He grabs the fabric of my dress and pulls it up until my knee is exposed. When his palm rests against my bare skin, I shudder. "I bet I could make you talk." His hand creeps up my thigh.

"Don't."

"That's better." He stops his progress and returns his palm to my knee. "I'd like for you to tell me your real name."

I look straight ahead at the piano. "The Prophet gave me my real name. Delilah."

He shrugs. "I suppose Delilah Roberts isn't such a terrible name, is it?"

When his hand starts to creep again, I say, "No, it's fine."

"You'll learn to like it... And me."

I turn and meet his light blue eyes. "Just because you buy me doesn't mean you own me."

"And there it is." He grips my knee. "That little bit of something extra. How have you managed to keep it in the Cloister?"

I silently curse myself for failing to play along. "I'm no different than the other Maidens."

He tsks. "Not true at all. You've got some fight. I like that." He shifts so I can feel his erection pressing against my ass. "I'm paying for that."

I try to edge away from him, but he holds me tight. "Stop."

"Fuck, I love it when you say that." He grabs my hair and presses his lips to mine. It's ugly—our teeth clacking and his tongue sliding across the seam of my mouth. I won't open for him. He pulls my hair harder, his other hand going to my throat.

I grab his wrist and dig my nails in.

He smiles against me. "More of that, my darling."

"Fuck you." I fight his grip, but he's far stronger. "You'll never have me."

"I'll have you so many ways." He yanks my head back. "You won't be able to move without thinking about the things I've done to you." His warm breath presses against my ear. "I can't wait for you to fight me, to beg and cry, to tell me no, and then give in."

"Never." I grit my teeth.

"Soon." He relents but doesn't let go of my hair. "But I came to see you again today because I'll be out of town for a bit. D.C. doesn't stop—not even for the holidays."

I narrow my eyes. "I'll cry every night."

He laughs, and it sends ugly chills racing through me.

"I'm sure you will. But when I get back, you'll be coming home with me. A New Year's gift for myself. I truly can't wait."

I want to tell him his "gift" has already been given to Adam, but I don't dare. My rebellion can never go that far. I can't risk Adam, not when he's working on a way out.

"My flight leaves in an hour." He sets me on the couch next to him, then rises.

I don't look at him, not even when he takes my hand and kisses the back. "Until next week, darling."

Movement catches my eye, and I find Adam standing in the doorway, his anger barely contained. I've never noticed the vein in his temple pulsing until right this second.

When Evan turns around, Adam's ire changes into a light, fake smile, which is somehow even scarier than the open murderous rage. He walks Evan out, but reappears quickly, rushes to me, and grabs me by the front of my dress, yanking me up hard.

I cry out as he shakes me. "Don't ever speak to your suitor that way again!" His voice carries, likely to the Prophet's ears, but I don't miss his grin or the quick squeeze of my hand or the faint brush of his lips against mine that I can feel all the way down to my toes.

CHAPTER 22

ADAM

"One of them wants mine?" Noah flops onto his couch and lets out an uncomfortable grunt as he reaches for his remote. Felix, his orange tabby, climbs into his lap and starts a loud purr.

"He's a mayor from Bay Minette. Small potatoes, but he comes from money, and has an eye for your girl." I kick my aching feet up onto his ottoman. "All day talking to these fucking perverts, and then Dad chimes in and reminds me he needs new stock for the Cathedral and the Chapel. There aren't enough Maidens to go around." I lean my head back. "How's the farm stuff?"

He flicks on the TV, which defaults to the Heavenly Channel—the Prophet Leon Monroe yapping nonstop.

"Turn that shit off." I feel around on his side table for the joint I saw when I walked in.

"Hang on." He presses a few buttons and the Cloister training room flickers onto the screen. "Damn, strap-on day."

I look for Delilah. She stands in the ring of Maidens, her eyes on the awkward ass-fucking the Spinner is directing.

"This should be hot." Noah points. "But it's the furthest thing from it."

I light up the joint and take a drag, then lean over and pass it to him. "Farm?" I remind him.

"Oh, yeah. Nothing I can do in the middle of winter except have the guys start clearing the trees and grinding the stumps." He pulls a puff of smoke into his mouth, then inhales. Felix's eyes begin to droop, already sleepy in his master's lap.

I don't particularly want to talk about farming or suitors, but that's what my father will be listening for. "There were actually two who wanted your girl, but the mayor has more cash, so he gets dibs. The other guy—owns some tractor place in Huntsville—can pick from the others."

"Dad change his mind about letting them go early?"

"No." I take the joint and inhale deeply before stubbing it out. "But he's happy to take deposits on them."

"What about yours?"

I blow the smoke out of my lungs and return my gaze to the screen. To her. "She's about to be bought and paid for." Forcing the next words from my lips is difficult, but necessary. "Which is good news for me, at least. I'll be rid of my Maiden duties. It's not like they're any fun since I can't mark her, can't even bruise her. So good riddance."

Noah raises an eyebrow but plays along. "You know, you could actually talk to her. She's more than just a sex—"

"No, that's all she is." Lies roll off my tongue, each one more bitter than the last. "A good ass-fuck, but I can't even get that going with her goddamn suitor breathing down my neck."

"Sorry, man." He shrugs and pets the dozing Felix.

I would ask about Gregory the lizard, but since he's supposed to be nothing more than ashes, I don't say a word. We've done our duty—made it look like we're carrying on with the Prophet's agenda as usual. The real conversation will take place outside, away from the microphones tucked away in our houses.

We'll plan our father's death under the cold stars that pay no mind to our machinations.

Delilah kneels as I enter her room. She's already nude, her pale skin almost glowing under the soft light from overhead. Her obedience sends a jolt of heat straight to my cock. I don't know if I would have been like this if it weren't for my upbringing, but I can't help the thrill her submission gives me.

I sit in front of her, and she moves closer without me even asking, her gray eyes focused on mine. "Hi."

I run my fingers through her hair, sifting the impossibly soft strands. She calms the storm that constantly rages inside me with nothing more than her presence and a softly whispered "hi."

"How do you do that?" I trace along her jaw with my fingertips.

"What?"

"Nothing." I let my fingers dance lower, grazing her collar bones and then venturing farther to the swells of her breasts.

Her lips part, a soft sigh on her breath as I stroke her hard nipple, the peak begging for my mouth.

"What did you learn today, little lamb?" I alternate between breasts, teasing one bud and then the next.

"I, um..." She makes an mmm noise and bites her lip.

"I didn't quite get that."

"We did this thing where, oh—"

I pinch her nipple. "Go on."

She shakes her head a tiny bit, as if trying to clear it. "It was these strap-ons."

"Did you wear one?" I slide my other hand down to her breasts, kneading each one, teasing the tips. They fill my palms perfectly, and the need to leave my bite marks on her skin roars up from my black depths.

"No, I just watched."

"Did you like it?"

That question snaps her head up. "Not in the least."

"Why not?" I squeeze her breasts to the point where she moans.

"Because they didn't want it. It wasn't um—"

"Consensual?"

"Right." She arches her back and I rub my palms up and down against her nipples.

"Is this?" I smirk as she wrinkles her nose.

"Depends on how you look at it." She presses her thighs together.

"And how do you look at it?"

"I'm trapped here, and you're the only man that gets to touch me, so there's coercion there."

"You wouldn't want me if it weren't for this arrangement?" Playing with her like this makes my dick so hard it nearly hurts.

She bites her lip again, her even little teeth pressing into the pink flesh. "I don't know."

I grab her by the waist and lift her, tossing her onto the bed. "I do."

She scrambles onto her back and stares at me wide-eyed as I yank my shirt over my head and reach for my belt.

"Spread your legs wide, little lamb."

"Adam."

I slide my belt from its loop and unbutton my pants, pushing them and my boxers to the floor.

She licks her lips as my cock pops free.

"Now!" I snap the belt into my palm.

Her legs slowly open, revealing the pink, wet perfection between her thighs. "What are you—" She cries out when the leather hits her sensitive skin.

"You think this is just coincidence?" I hit her again, the leather reddening her pussy with clear marks. "Wider!"

She grips the sheets, and her knees shake as she scoots her heels farther apart. I hit her again, this time with a little less force. Her squeal makes my balls ache, and I'm desperate to fuck her, to take what I can't have again and again until it's mine.

"Well?" I strike her again.

"No!" She shakes her head.

"Arch your back." I toss the belt and climb on top of her, needing to do what I've been imaging to her milky-white tits. With a firm bite next to her nipple, I leave my mark as she squirms beneath me.

"Adam." Her gasp urges me onward, and I bite her other breast as my cock presses against her hot pussy. Fuck, my head is so close. I could fuck her again. Could give us both what we need. I want it so bad that I have to back off.

She watches me with heavy-lidded eyes, and I know she's desperate for the same thing I am. When she crawls onto her knees, then lowers her head and licks her own wetness from my tip, I can't stop myself. I wrap my fingers in her hair and pull her forward. My cock slides into her throat. She grips my thighs, her nails digging in, but I don't release her. I need this control, and I've never tasted anything sweeter than dominion over my little lamb.

When I finally push her back, she gasps for air, her eyes watering as she looks up at me.

"Again." I pull her onto my cock, her throat taking me, squeezing me in her heat. Giving her some room to move, I back off. She wraps one small hand around the base of my cock and sucks me hard, her cheeks hollowing out as she bobs her head.

My balls draw up close to me as she sucks and strokes, her hand working in conjunction with her mouth. She gives me head with a recklessness that stirs every dark desire I've ever had for her. The slight graze of her teeth sends me higher, my body coiling like a snake.

"Stop." I grab her hair and pull her off my cock, her lips swollen and wet. Lying on the bed, I pull her on top of me and move her up until her pussy hovers above my face. "Suck me." I can barely understand my own voice, and I don't give a shit. I just have to taste her. And I do. With one lick, I get the flavor of her needy cunt, and I need more.

Gripping her hips, I press her to my face as she takes my cock in her warm mouth. She moans around it, and I slap her ass, urging her onward as I suck and lick all of her wet flesh, then move to her asshole.

Her legs tremble as I lick her hole, taunting the ridged skin with the tip of my tongue before returning to her clit. She picks up her pace, her body rocking on top of mine as she takes my cock deeper into her throat with each stroke. I light up her ass with another slap and press my tongue into her tight pussy. It's not allowed, but I've already broken the biggest rule. Feeling her from the inside with my tongue is just one of my many smaller transgressions.

She seizes on my head, sucking and probing with her velvet tongue. *Fuck.* I'll be damned if I come before she does, no matter how hard she's trying to get me there. I switch my focus to her clit, lashing it with my tongue as she moans and takes me deeper into her mouth. When her legs start to shake, I know I have her. Her mouth goes slack around my cock, and I press my teeth against her clit. Her body stills, and her moan comes from somewhere deep inside her. I jab my tongue inside her again and feel the waves of contractions from her hot pussy, then I move back to her clit, licking all the pleasure out of her and into my mouth.

When she quiets and returns to my cock, it doesn't take long. I don't give her any warning when my load surges up my shaft, and I thrust my hips up. She latches her lips around me, sucking as I empty into her mouth. The release is blinding, absolute. I groan and squeeze her ass, my face still buried in her cunt. She swallows and uses her tongue to scoop the last bit of come from the tip of my cock. After it's over, she lays her head on my thigh, her body heaving as she gulps in air. I kiss her pussy, her ass, everywhere my lips can reach, then grab her and pull her around, laying her head on my chest.

Covered in sweat, we lie together, our heartbeats slowly settling down.

She says something, but her voice is too muffled for me to hear. I pull her up so her head rests in the crook of my neck.

"What, little lamb?"

"He's coming for me on Wednesday. Less than a week. Is there a plan?"

"There is." I stroke the strands of hair from her damp forehead and whisper in her ear. "Tuesday night at the Temple. Don't drink the wine. Don't eat the fruit."

She nods. "Anything else?"

"Nothing you need to know. Just be ready."

"Okay." She relaxes on top of me, her body molding to mine with each passing moment. I wish I could stay, could hold her as she falls asleep. But that's not possible, not here.

Snuggling even closer, she kisses my neck. "It's not coincidence. You and me. We're not..." She sighs against my ear, an angel's breath warming her demon. "We'd be like this even if we weren't here. I'd be yours no matter where we were."

I kiss her forehead and let the emotion that I don't dare name flow between us. It's the one tie that no power on heaven or earth can sever, but it's so fragile in this place that speaking it aloud will surely destroy it.

CHAPTER 23

DELILAH

"Delilah, you're with Miriam this morning." Grace grabs me from the line of Maidens headed to training.

Eve shoots me a concerned look, but continues walking as Grace pulls me past the training room and toward the wing of the Cloister where the Spinners live. I've rarely been over this way, the most memorable time being when Grace took me to her office and broke my finger.

"Best behavior." Venom infuses her words. "I don't want some stupid bitch like you making me look bad to Miriam."

"You don't need my help to do that." It was supposed to be just a thought. It wasn't.

She halts and shoves me against the wall. "Maybe you think you've got Adam fooled so you're untouchable. Is that it? I guarantee you that's not the case. The Cloister is mine. I will do whatever I have to do to keep all you cunts in line."

I don't push back. I've already done enough.

"One more word from you, and I'll break all your fingers and scar your face."

I swallow, my mouth going dry.

"Don't think I'll do it? Just ask that dyke Chastity." She backs off and shoves me down the hall.

I walk ahead of her, my thoughts roiling. I'd often wondered about the scar on Chastity's forehead but assumed it was from some accident. Did Grace put it there out of spite?

"Stop." She points to a closed door. "Here."

I open it to find Miriam seated at a long conference table with cushy leather chairs. A white binder sits in front of her, and an uncharacteristically sour look mars her face. "You're late."

"Apologies. We were just—"

"I don't need your excuses. You—" She points at me. "Sit down. You—" She flicks her wrist at Grace. "Get out."

Grace bristles, but doesn't bite. She closes the door as I take a chair across from Miriam. Wearing a high-necked forest-green dress, she appears to be following the Prophet's strict new edict on women's appearance.

I fold my hands in my lap and drop my gaze, doing my best to look like the obedient Maiden she expects.

"Cut that shit out. You're giving me the creeps." She flips open her binder, and I look up as she pages through several sheets of paper. "We're here to discuss your placement with Senator Roberts. You'll skip training for the rest of the week. The Prophet asked the senator to tell us if he has any preferences for you—as in if he wants you silent, or trained in the whip, or delivered with a butt plug, or what—but he didn't specify anything. Just wants you as you are." She gives me an appraising glance. "Though I don't know why. Anyway, that's not an entirely bad thing, since it'll give us more time to talk through what's expected of you as a senator's wife, but first and foremost, as one of the Prophet's chosen."

I shift in my seat. The way she speaks makes the idea of being Evan's wife a little too real. Queasy, I take a deep breath and try to calm myself.

She looks at her French tips, far more interested in them than me. "The Prophet asked me here as a special favor. I don't like being away from Montgomery too long —and this is something you need to learn too—because when I'm away from the governor for more than a day or two, his interest in me can wane. That's unacceptable. Your training is intended to make sure you're always what your husband wants, always open to try what he suggests. By making yourself invaluable in the bedroom, you solidify your place next to your husband. Understand?"

"I think so but—"

"Good." She ignores me and flips a page in the binder. "Your guy is thirty-five, handsome, and from what we've gleaned at the Chapel—really into power play. Never married, a big up-and-comer in D.C., and known to visit certain sex clubs under an alias. Now, tell me how you intend to use this information to better the Prophet." She looks up at me expectantly.

I'm a kid in school, naked, and without my homework done. "I, um... I would—"

She rolls her eyes. "Why'd he have to pick a dumb one?" Utterly gone is the beauty queen façade. Here, she's all business and fully invested in the Prophet and his message—and particularly shrewd about it. "Let me ask that in a way someone like you can understand." She laces her fingers together on top of the binder. "From what I've just told you, what tools do you have in your arsenal to please your husband?"

I grab the low-hanging fruit. "Perfect obedience?"

"Jesus." She shakes her head at me like I'm an utter idiot. "Perfect obedience is for all the stupid sheep, not for us."

I don't point out that she's wearing granny clothes solely based on the Prophet's teaching of "perfect obedience."

"Look, your guy is into power play. That means he wants to feel challenged, but in the end, he wants to be in control."

"So you want me to challenge him?" At least that comes naturally, though this entire prep session is just a hypothetical. I'll never belong to Evan Roberts.

"Obviously." She sighs. "Fight him a little. Give him something he feels he has to overcome. That sort of thing excites him. Then let him be alpha and do whatever he wants with you."

"Okay." *So not okay.*

"But that's not what's important."

"It's important to *me*."

"Listen, Mary or Sharon or whatever your name is—there is no 'you'." Her eyes harden, and she reminds me of a predatory bird, some sort of hawk. "Not anymore. Everything you are belongs to the Prophet. You exist only to further his goals. You owe everything you have to him. It doesn't matter what Evan Roberts does to your body. He can fuck you, cut you, hurt you, do whatever his little depraved heart desires. And you will let him do it because it pleases him. Pleasing him is your job, because by pleasing him, you can please the Prophet."

I cross my arms over my chest and return her icy glare. "What else?"

"You're finally getting it." She drums her nails on the table. "Once you get him where you want by being the perfect sex toy, he'll feel comfortable to share things with you. Pillow talk. About what he's doing in D.C., dirty secrets, desires, plans. All of that information is what you will send back to the Prophet. Understand?"

"So, I'm a spy."

"Don't get ahead of yourself." Her tone grows more conspiratorial. "First you have to get his trust by fucking him the way he likes. Men are easy like that. If they want you, they trust you. So you have to keep the bedroom hot at all times. That's how you'll get him to share information with you. And after that—once you've proven your worth—the Prophet will give you instructions."

"Like what?"

"You'll see. But, usually, it involves nudging your husband in the right direction."

"You mean nudging him to do something to benefit the Prophet?"

"Oh, look who's not as dumb as she seems." She smirks.

"This is how you live as the governor's wife? Perfect fuck toy, obedient wife, but a spy for the Prophet?"

She looks away, finally, staring at an empty corner of the room. "I do what I have to do to serve the Prophet." The snark is gone from her tone, replaced by a bone-aching sort of tired that seems too heavy for her to bear.

"Don't you ever want anything for yourself?"

She whips her head back around, her brief moment of honesty fading behind a thin smile. "I don't need anything except the Prophet's love and approval. He gives me plenty of both, and I'm guaranteed a spot at his right hand in our heavenly home."

"He tells you you're his favorite, doesn't he? He told me the same thing. That I'm chosen, that I'm special. He tells all of us the—"

She leans forward, her eyes narrowing. "But with me, he *means* it. Don't mistake your place. I don't care if you marry the president, you aren't above me. You'll see. I am truly chosen."

Some delusions are far too strong to be broken.

Eve sits next to me at lunch, her knee knocking against

mine beneath the table. I glance up, scanning the room for any Spinners who might be looking our way.

"Sarah." That one word in Eve's broken whisper haunts me, and I have to take a deep breath to fight off the tears.

"I know." I squeeze her hand.

She leans even closer. "What is the Father of Fire? Does he mean the devil? Did he send Sarah to hell?" Her urgent whispers cut me.

I glance up to make sure the Spinners aren't watching before responding. "I think he believes he speaks to the devil, yeah. But that's just crazy talk, like everything else here."

"The fire. Did you see it?"

"Fire does stuff like that." I've been telling myself the same thing ever since I witnessed the vortex of flames behind the Prophet. It was nothing. "Doesn't mean anything. Sarah's not in hell." I don't even believe in hell, but that's beside the point.

"I can't stay here." She forks a limp piece of broccoli, but doesn't eat it.

"Don't do anything that could—" I halt my words as a Spinner turns toward us. Taking a big bite of my greens, I chew the unseasoned mush until the Spinner looks away again. I swallow the lump and continue, "Don't try anything."

"Why not?" Her grip hardens on my hand. "They'll kill me or make me a whore or send me to hell with Sarah. I'd rather try to get away than—" She yelps.

"Separate!" Grace grabs Eve by the collar and drags

her to another, empty table. "There is no talking, and no one is above the rules." She hits Eve on the upper arm. "Understood?"

"Yes." Eve cowers as Grace storms back over to me. "From now on, you eat alone. You speak to no one. I will not allow you to poison these Maidens against me!" Her mouth twists in fury as she raises her baton.

I cover my head and wait for the blow.

"No marks." Abigail calls from the kitchen window. "Not on that one. You going to disobey the Prophet?"

Everyone in the room stills, even Grace. She glares at the old Spinner, but lowers her baton, then sheaths it in her belt. "Eat! And you—" She points at Abigail. "See me in my office once your lunch duty is done."

"Of course, Grace." Abigail returns to scrubbing the pass-through window, ignoring whatever daggers Grace still throws at her as she storms from the dining room.

I sit up, shame coloring my cheeks at the way I cowered.

Once Grace is gone, Susannah reaches toward me, grasping for Eve's tray. I push it toward her, and she snags it and transfers it to Eve's table. Eve clutches her arm, silent tears streaming down her face.

Chastity emerges from the kitchen, a tray of rolls in her hands. My mouth waters at the sight. Bread! How long has it been since we've had anything even resembling the simple deliciousness of bread? The Prophet wants to keep us lean, which Grace says is the form "most pleasing to the Lord," so carbs are quite a rebellion.

"I baked them last night, so they're a bit old." She

hands them out around the room, the Maidens taking greedy bites.

When I get mine, I do the same, and I almost moan at how good it is. Cold, a little stale, and absolutely perfect. I want to scoop more off the tray, to hoard the dwindling supply for myself.

Chastity visits Eve last, surreptitiously sneaking her two rolls instead of one. She leans over and whispers something in her ear, but I can't hear it, before disappearing back into the kitchen. Abigail hasn't looked up at all since Grace left, intentionally ignorant of the contraband bread.

Eve takes a roll in her palm, sniffs it, then bites. Her eyes close, and she's in bread nirvana with the rest of us.

My roll is long gone, and I peer at the kitchen window. I want to warn Chastity that Tuesday night is important, that we have a real chance of escape. But I can't get to her. And a shadow creeps across my mind— can I trust her? Would she turn us in? I don't think so, but that doesn't mean I should take the risk of alerting her something's coming. She'll know when it happens. *If* it happens.

Then again, I know she has more information on Georgia. This may be my last chance to find out what happened to her. I want to leave here, to destroy the Prophet and all he's working for, but I can't let go of the thread that brought me here in the first place. So many times, I've wanted to ask Adam about her. Even though I feel in my heart that he wasn't the one who killed her, what if I'm wrong? I don't know if I could bear it. A flash of him with the knife at Sarah's—no, Georgia's—throat bursts through my mind, and the bread threatens to come back up.

If I confess to him, it could just muddy the waters and ruin our escape attempt, which hovers on the edge of disaster already. I have no illusions that Adam's plan won't result in bloodshed. There's no way he can save me or himself from the Prophet without violence.

The forbidden bread reassures me that Chastity will fight for us and for herself. I just hope the rest of the Maidens will see the opening and do what they must to regain their freedom.

And even if they aren't ready to fight, I am.

CHAPTER 24

ADAM

"You decided what we're going to do about Davis?" Noah leans against the side of the Cloister, a cigarette dangling from his lips.

I take a spot next to him as he passes the smoke. Pulling in a lungful of nicotine, I hold it, then let it go in a white plume. "I'm still thinking." I can taste the alcohol on the filter, but I already smelled it on Noah when I walked up.

He raises a bruised brow. "You're actually considering wearing a wire?"

"Hell no." I stuff my hands into my pockets. "I don't narc. You know that." I've been toying with the idea, even if I tell Noah otherwise. Wearing a wire would be simple, and I could catch my father saying any number of illegal things at any time. But, everything he says will also implicate Noah and me. That's not an outcome I will accept, especially when Davis doesn't have the authority to offer us full immunity.

"Then what?"

"I always look for a way to play both ends against the middle." I shrug and shift from one aching foot to the next.

"You found a way to do that here?"

"Not yet." I motion for the cigarette and take the last hit. "But I will."

"I can't believe that douche is FBI." He crosses his arms over his chest. "Threatening us with prison time."

"He doesn't have a thing on us or we'd already be busted and over a barrel. The most he's got is me beating his ass and our breaking and entering his house—but he won't do shit about that. It would blow his cover."

"Right." He scrubs a hand down his jaw, the bristles loud in the quiet night. "I guess we need to backburner him and think about Tuesday."

"Tuesday." I nod. "You know what to do. Just be prepared. It's going to get a lot worse before it gets better."

"What if..." He swallows hard. "What if it comes down to it, and I'm the one who has to... you know, kill Dad. I don't know if I can do—"

"I'll handle that. You just watch your back and make sure none of the Protectors get out of that room. Then we'll fight our way to Mom. Once we've got her and Delilah, we're out."

"And after?" His light blue eyes are inscrutable as he stares at me. "What then?"

"Anything. Anything we can think of. We'll have money and freedom. We can go wherever we want."

"Anywhere?" His reticence gives way to a note of hope.

"Yes." I can't help but smile at the idea. Real freedom. "After Tuesday, we are free to have our own lives, to be different people—the people we would have been if it weren't for this place."

His smile is wistful. "I like the sound of that. Maybe we can move to, I don't know, like an island or something? In the Caribbean?"

"With the money I've stashed, we can buy our own island if we want."

He smiles, finally, his grin boyish and warm. "I'll name it Noahland and give Felix and Gregory the run of the place."

"Good to know you still have the ambitions of a sixteen-year-old." I clap him on the shoulder and laugh when he winces. "Pussy."

"Dick," he mutters as Zion walks up.

Zion smirks at Noah, probably admiring the bruises he put on my brother's face.

Once he's inside, Noah turns to me. "Now that's one guy I won't mind putting down for good."

"That's the spirit." I can't deny my need to see Delilah any longer. Pushing off the wall, I stride to the door, Noah at my back. We walk the long hallway to the dormitories and separate.

When I walk in, Delilah is on her knees, her head slightly bowed. For the first time in my life, I actually feel lucky. To have a woman like this waiting for me is something I never expected, and I certainly don't deserve it. I stride over to her and sit.

She rests her cheek on my knee, and I stroke her hair.

"What training did you get up to today, little lamb?" I feather my fingers across her neck.

"I had a special session with Miriam."

My usual scorn for the woman churns inside me. "And what pearls of wisdom did the First Lady of Alabama have to offer?"

"She told me that even if I'm married to Evan, that my true responsibility is to the Prophet."

I nod along. "That's correct."

"And as long as I serve Evan in whatever ways he wants—" My fists clench, but she continues on, "And submit to him as his wife in every way, that I'll—"

"That's enough." I yank her off the floor and slam her on the bed.

She smiles as I pin her hands above her head.

Has a woman's smile ever intrigued a man more? Not even the *Mona Lisa* has anything on Delilah at this moment. "Toying with me, little lamb?"

She bats her lashes. "I have to use whatever leverage I have, don't I?"

I smirk and lower my mouth to her throat, biting hard and then licking my teeth marks. "You're playing a dangerous game."

"We all are," she whispers.

I kiss to her ear. "Tuesday. There will be violence, blood, and chaos. I need you to stick with me, understand? Don't put yourself in danger, but stay by my side if you can. We're getting out of this hell. But we'll have to pay with blood. Hopefully, not ours."

"I'm ready." She kisses my jaw, her soft lips warm against me, then stops.

"What?" I pull back and stare into her impossibly gray eyes.

"I... Need to ask you something."

Foreboding whips across my soul like a harsh wind. "What?"

"Closer." She glances toward the vent.

I let go of her hands and wrap my arms around her, pinning her to me. "Ask."

She's tense, so different from the playfulness just a moment ago. "Okay, I just need to... Give me a second." She seems to wrestle with how to continue, her silence unnerving me.

Her breathing speeds up. "Um." She shifts beneath me.

I sit up and pull her into my lap. Holding her tight, I nestle her head in the crook of my neck. I want her close, and the foreboding from earlier hits me even harder.

Goosebumps pebble her skin, and I whip her blanket up and wrap it around her.

"Thanks." She lets out a tight breath. "Okay, did you know a..." She clears her throat and blurts out, "Do you know if your father has a book?"

"A book?"

"One that he wrote himself with different sorts of symbols in—"

"Yes, you mean *the* book." I wonder who told her about it, but I don't ask.

"Right. Have you seen it?"

"This is what you wanted to ask me about?" I don't pretend to understand where she's going with her questions, but something tells me she's veering off from her main intent.

"Have you seen it?"

I let her deflect for the moment. "Rarely. He keeps it locked away, and only gets it out for special occasions." I don't want to elaborate on the last *special occasion*. My hands are still covered with blood from it, though no one else can see it but me.

"Is he the only one with access to it?"

"Yes."

"Are you sure?"

I pull her away from my ear and try to find her in the gray of her eyes. "Why are you asking this?"

"I just need to know. Are you sure no one else can..." She lets her words trail off.

I nod and pull her close again. "It's in his desk in the house in a locked drawer. He has the only key."

"Have you ever used it? The book, I mean?"

"Used it?" Now I'm even more lost than before. "How would I use a book full of delusional ranting and doodles?"

"To, I don't know, copy the marks onto something or onto—"

"Someone?" Her question becomes clear. "You want to know who put the markings on Sarah?" I don't feel like

I have the right to say the girl's name. It's profane on my lips, as if I'm marring her more than I already have.

"Yes."

"Only my father touches the book. It would have had to been him."

"Not you?" I can barely hear her now. "Not ever?"

"Not me. Not ever." I don't let her questions sting me. She's right to ask them. Maybe, if it weren't for Delilah, I would have been the one to hurt Sarah by carving the marks into her skin. I've done so many terrible things that I can't say for sure one way or the other.

"Good." She finally lets go of most of her tension, melting into my arms.

"Was that all you wanted to know?" I hold her, not caring what the camera sees. Maybe my father will call me in for being too easy on my Maiden, but I'll take the punishment.

She hesitates, then wraps her arms around my neck. "That was all."

My soul settles, though a nagging doubt still rattles around inside me. What was her true question?

When I leave Delilah's room, Grace is waiting in the hallway, her face pinched.

"What?" I stride past her. My feet have fucking had it for the day, but I'll be damned if I show any weakness in front of her.

She hurries to follow me into the long hall. "Can you meet me later?"

"The fuck?" I don't care what she wants. Nothing she says is going to change anything. I just want to get to my place, turn on the video of Delilah, smoke a joint, and fall asleep. None of that includes Grace.

She grabs my elbow, but I shake her off and enter the door code to get out.

"Wait!" She dogs my steps as I walk into the night. "Adam, please."

I keep going.

"It's about your mother," she hisses.

I stop. "What did you say?"

"I need to talk to you about your mother. Tonight. Please?"

She's playing a game. She has to be. But she's dangled the right bait, and now I have to bite. "Why can't you just say it now?"

She shakes her head. "Tonight. In the punishment circle. Midnight."

I grab a handful of her dress right below her throat and shake her. "If this is some sort of stupid trick to—"

"It's not!" she squeaks. "I swear."

Footsteps behind me have me releasing her.

Abigail, the oldest Spinner, hurries past and enters the door code.

Grace turns her sharp eye on the woman. "What are you doing out this late?"

"Had to order some things for the larder and forgot to do it earlier." She misses the code and tries again.

Grace gives me one more look. "Midnight," she whispers. Then she turns and follows Abigail inside, berating her all the way.

I lean my head back and stare at the crescent moon that peers at me from behind wispy clouds. If Grace crosses me tonight, I can't guarantee that I won't drag her to the creek and drown her just like I've fantasized about a million times. Not even Delilah's calming influence can abate the rage I have for that treacherous bitch, and I doubt anything ever will.

The moon is higher now, the clouds dissolving under its light. I keep my hands stuffed in my pockets, a pistol warming against my right palm. Leaning against a tree at the edge of the punishment clearing, I wait for Grace to show.

The ground is still scuffed in the spot where I beat Davis not that long ago, the three sturdy crosses at the edge of the clearing casting their moon shadow along the indentations in the dirt.

I can't feel the tip of my nose, and the time is ticking past midnight. I've almost decided to leave when I hear an engine on the main road of the compound. The headlights are off, but I can see the black Mercedes creeping along the gravel road, the tires crunching loud in the quiet night.

When it stops, Grace exits the passenger side. I can't see the driver, and I don't like that one fucking bit.

She hurries to the center of the clearing, her gaze sweeping around but not finding me. I could leave now, just disappear into the night and leave her. Foolishly, I don't.

I whistle as I step from behind a wide pine and walk to her, but I keep my peripheral vision on the car.

"You're here." She states the obvious like a real pro.

"What do you want?" I cast a direct glance to the sedan. "Who's driving?"

"I'm so glad you're here." She beams, and I can see the slightest glimpse of the innocent girl I broke so many years ago. It disgusts me. Just like I disgust me.

"Get on with it."

She motions to the car. The engine dies, and I grip my gun tighter, pulling it to the edge of my pocket. When the door opens and Castro steps out, I pull the gun all the way, leveling it at him.

"Adam, wait." Grace doesn't touch me, but hovers right at my elbow as Castro shoots me a surly glare, then walks to the back door and opens it.

My hand falters and drops when my mother steps out.

CHAPTER 25

ADAM

*G*ut punched, I watch as Castro leads my mother to the middle of the circle.

"Adam." She reaches out and pulls me to her, the same scent rushing to my nose that I remember from my childhood—some sort of floral soap or perfume that I've never smelled anywhere else.

"Mom." I bring her in close. "What is this?" My mind starts churning before I'm over the shock. If she can get out like this, maybe taking her and Delilah away from here will be easier than I thought. Maybe I can do it tonight, right now. Maybe—

"Adam." She rubs my back, then lets me go. "We have plans, and it's time you knew about them."

"Plans?" I can't take my eyes off her. She's here, real, and no one to stop me from whisking her away—except Castro. But I have no problem dropping him and leaving him for the Protectors to find.

He takes my mother's elbow, but not roughly, not in his usual asshole sort of way.

"What the fuck is going on?" I glance to the tree line, amazed that Noah hasn't broken cover and come out here to marvel right along with me, but he's staying put just like I told him.

"We don't have long before I'm missed." Mom stares up at me, her eyes the same blue as Noah's, though it's hard to tell in the moonlight. "The Father of Fire has spoken to me, and I know that a new Prophet will rise very soon. We've worked hard to make this happen. It's been in the works for years." She smooths her hands down my arms. "And we know that you are the perfect successor to your father's seat. You will be the new Prophet. The Father of—"

"What?" I understand her words, but I have no idea what she's saying. "What are you talking about? The Father of Fire? That's not real. None of this is. Mom." I take her shoulders. "What's wrong with you? If you can get free this easily, why haven't you come to me before? We could have been away from here a long time ago. We need to go—"

"Go?" She shakes her head, her gray hair dull though her eyes shine. "We can't leave. This is where we belong. All of this should be ours. And it *can* be. With you as the new Prophet, the compound can be something we're proud of. Somewhere the faithful can be free."

"Free? Here?" I grip her harder. "Mom, there's no way to be free here. This is a prison. Every bit of it needs to be burned to the ground."

"Let her go, *pendejo*." Castro edges closer.

"It's fine." She pats him on the stomach. "Don't worry. My son would never harm me."

"And what's he got to do with this?" I snarl. "He lets Dad hurt you. He—"

"And you don't?" She may as well have slapped me.

I recoil and try to understand the person standing in front of me, but nothing is making sense.

"Just listen to her." Grace moves closer to her side, the three of them staring me down. "We have a plan. Everything is already in motion. We've already given the Father of Fire a great sacrifice. He was so pleased with it that he's shown us the way. It's taken time, but we're almost there, at the cusp. And we did it for you, Adam. So you can be the Prophet."

My head spins, but I hang on to a single piece of what Grace said. "What sacrifice?"

Grace drops her gaze.

My mother reaches out again and takes my hand. "It doesn't matter."

"It matters to me. What have you done?"

Mom shrugs, as if she's confessing to nothing more than an inadvertent mistake. "Just one of your father's harlots. A girl. She was Noah's Maiden. The one with the blonde hair—"

"Georgia."

She nods. "Her."

"You mutilated her, then killed her." I can't tell if I'm asking a question or making a statement.

"We did." Mom says it so calmly, as if we're speaking

about dinner plans or current events, not the ruthless murder of an innocent. "It was so easy to lure her away. She kept talking about seeing her sister—until Castro tied her up." She looks at her hands, the skin thinner now and spotted with age. "I didn't know I could do it. Cut her throat. But it was so easy. Easier than I ever imagined."

I clench my eyes shut, trying to set my world to rights when it is so, so wrong. I don't know what to say. There's nothing left. She's gone. Whatever light she had in her when I was young has been beaten, tortured, and ground out of her. Now there is only darkness—the same shades that paint my father.

She is lost.

And I am in mourning. For her, for myself, for the life we could have had. Blinking, I open my eyes and look into hers. I don't see my mother. She's gone somewhere so far and so deep that I'll never be able to reach her.

"Adam." She speaks with my mother's voice, but she is not my mother. "We had to. For you. Don't you see? Everything we've done was for you. This is your chance to take what's yours! Get rid of your father. Keep this place for yourself and your brother. You could make it pure again. Lead the people into the light. Show the Father of Fire why you deserve to be a king among men." She pauses and turns her head to the right, looking through the trees toward the Cathedral. "We'll have to do something about your father's other whores and their bastards, but that can come later."

Everything goes numb, and though my mother continues speaking, her words don't make it through to me. My mother would never hurt anyone, especially not some young girl with her whole life ahead of her, and not *children*. But this creature isn't my mother, I remind myself.

"—and once you're the Prophet, I'll be able to help you with the public side, guiding you as your mother. Noah will fall in line, as will the rest of the Protectors, and Castro can deal with anyone who gets out of hand. He'll be your number one Protector and my companion. All the men will have to swear a new oath to you, and we'll probably need to tighten the reins a bit at first to make sure they are obedient. But all the rest can continue —building Monroeville, consolidating our people under one umbrella, using them to work the land and make us self-sufficient. We'll still allow several of them with high-paying jobs to work off-compound and increase their tithes in increments." She tsks. "That's something your father never understood. He wants them all here, but that doesn't make sense when we can pull money from out *there*." She takes a deep breath. "I'm rambling, but I'm just so excited to start this new chapter." She takes my hands again, though I can barely feel her touch. "Just think of it—you, me, Noah, all of us a happy family again."

"And Dad?"

"We'll deal with him, Castro and me. His time is almost at hand." Her voice comes to me as if through a tunnel.

"When?"

"Don't you worry about that. I want you focused on

the future of this place." She smooths her clammy palms down my cheeks. "You, son, are the future."

"We're cutting it close." Castro taps his watch.

"We must go." She hugs me tight. "But remember what I've said. Your time is almost here. I love you, Adam."

"Now, ma'am." Castro tugs at her elbow.

She pats my cheek one more time and lets him lead her away to the car.

"It's the future, Adam. It can be our future." Grace moves close. "We can start over. I want to give you another child, to show you that we can have everything we ever wanted. I made a mistake with... Well, before. But this time I'll do better. This time, with a new little girl, we can be—"

"If you don't get out of my sight, I will drag you to the creek and do everything I've promised you. Understand?"

She cringes and backs away. "You'll see, Adam. I can be what you want. I'll show you."

Grace turns and scampers to the car, shooting me a glance before dropping into the passenger seat. After a few moments, they're gone. The night is still again, not even the air stirring—and it's as if they were never here at all.

Some leaves crunch to my left, and Noah appears from the shadowy woods, his steps rushed. "What the fuck, man? What. The. Fuck?" His eyes are wide.

"I don't know, but please tell me you have a cigarette."

He pulls one out of his pocket, his fingers shaking.

When he drops it, he kneels to retrieve it and finally gets it lit.

"Did you hear all of it?" I take it from his grasp and draw the burn into my lungs. My old habit is becoming new again.

"That you're the new Prophet and they're going to kill Dad? Yeah, I heard." His voice trembles. Maybe from cold. More likely from shock.

"Mom killed that girl. The one who went missing."

"Georgia, though she was Mary when she was mine." He pauses for a moment, and something like regret crosses his face. "I just assumed Dad—"

"I did, too. The markings on her couldn't have come from anywhere else."

"Yeah." He wrinkles his forehead with thought. "But he *did* have us out searching for her."

"He claimed she must have run away and was hiding somewhere on the compound." I dredge up the memories from that time, how angry Dad was when we couldn't find her, and how he went nuclear when an outsider found her body and made a stink. "After she was found, I figured he'd been acting and that he'd killed her all along."

"Right." He takes the cigarette from me. "Or at least I thought that was right. But Mom must have gotten the book. Or maybe, I don't know, maybe she came up with her own symbols. She said she's been talking—"

"To the devil. Yeah, I heard." I rub my eyes. So fucked—everything is utterly beyond fucked. "She could have come to us. For years now, we could have taken her and gone." Too many emotions crowd through me, but there's a little extra room for rage. Always has been. "This whole time, she's been sitting back and watching what's happening all because she wants to be the one to run this place with me as her puppet."

"She's still our mom." He puts a hand on my shoulder.

I shrug him off. "Just like the Prophet is still our dad?"

He frowns at the ground. "It's all so messed up."

"No shit." I take the last pull from the cigarette, then toss the butt.

"What do we do?"

I'm out of options. "We carry on with the plan."

"But Mom doesn't want to leave. How can we bring her?"

"I don't know, but we can't leave her here, especially if she wants to keep this place going. We have to take her with us one way or another." A pounding headache sets up shop behind my temples.

"What if she won't come?"

"Then we *make* her come by whatever means necessary."

"Adam." He grips my upper arm. "We can't hurt her. She's our mom."

"She killed an innocent girl after torturing her, Noah. *Your* Maiden."

He winces.

I keep going, "She thinks she talks to the devil. She's joined forces with that piece of shit, Castro. If she gets her wish, this place will be as bad or worse than it was under Dad." I point through the trees toward the east. "Did you hear what she had to say about the innocent children at the Cathedral?"

"She didn't say she would—"

"There's no coming back from where she is, Noah." I rub my forehead. "Have you learned nothing from Dad? When he started all this, there was no way to stop him. Remember?"

He furrows his brow, but slowly nods. "Yeah."

"It's the same delusion all over again. She's poisoned, just like he is. And they'd rather die from the poison than save themselves."

He shakes his head. "We can help her. Just hold off on this Tuesday plan and let me talk to her, or talk to Castro. I don't know. But hold off."

"I can't."

He throws his hands up. "Because of that fairy girl, some random piece of ass?"

My fist flies before I even think about it. Noah staggers back, one hand going to his jaw as he stares at me, eyes wide. I've never hit him before. Not like this.

I step toward him. "Noah—"

"Fuck off." He stands his ground, anger radiating from him.

"Please, I didn't mean to—"

"Don't fucking touch me!" he yells and puts all his frustration and despair of the last twenty minutes into it.

"Shit." I hang my head.

He lowers his voice, but the anger still bubbles in

each syllable. "You have to call it off. Give Mom a chance. Maybe she can end this without as much bloodshed. She said you could turn the Protectors to work for you. We don't have to kill them. Maybe she's right. We—"

"I can't let Delilah go to that senator. I can't." The thought of what he plans to do to her almost brings me to my knees.

"You'd choose her over your own blood?" He stops rubbing his jaw and scowls at me. "Her over *me*?"

"It's not like that, and you know it."

He shakes his head.

"Don't do this, Noah." I take another step toward him but he backs up. "We were together on this. I can't do it without you."

"No." He walks backward. "I'm out."

"Noah!" I rush toward him.

He lets a fist fly, catching me off-guard. I stumble and stop, the pain in my face dulling the ache in my feet.

"You chose wrong, big brother." He shakes his hand out, then turns and walks away into the gloom.

CHAPTER 26

*A*nother crash breaks the stillness of the early morning hour, and I suspect Adam has just destroyed something priceless in his house next door.

I take another drink from my bottle, not even tasting whatever liquor I've chosen for the evening's numbing session.

Felix sits on the ottoman, staring at me as I sit on the couch in the dark. His eyes are just visible in the light from the kitchen, giving a ghostly reflection back if he turns his head just right.

"What?" I ask him and take another swig. "What am I supposed to do?"

He doesn't answer, just keeps his post.

"Gregory is more useful than you. You know that? And he's a fucking lizard." My words are slurred, and I doubt anyone listening in could figure out what the fuck I'm saying, but I'm still present enough to keep my voice down.

Why can't I just sleep? I smoked up, drank up, and tried for the sweet oblivion of unconsciousness, but it won't come.

The sound of shattering glass punctures my hazy thoughts. "That sounded expensive." I chuckle, but not out of anything approaching humor.

"Faith, you know?" I keep talking to Felix, probably because he's the only one dumb enough to listen to me. "That's where this all started." I point toward Adam's house. "Faith." I nod, and Felix settles down into what I call the 'bunny look', his feet tucked beneath him, his eyes still alert. "I loved that little girl, too, you know? I loved her so much. But I believed, I had to believe, that what happened was God's plan. Right? Right. Because Dad told me so. And I went along. But Adam, something in him went wrong the day she died. And it's never going to be right again. You know?"

Felix blinks slowly.

"Before, he'd do what he was told, and wouldn't bite back. But after her, he became vicious." I take another long draw, surprised to find the bottle empty. "Fuck." I toss it away, and it rolls across the rug and under a chair.

Felix follows its trajectory, but doesn't make a move.

I close my eyes and see golden hair and a warm smile. "Mary. No, Georgia. Georgia was her name." My heart seems to squeeze to a halt. "She was so..." I flail for the right word. "Sweet. No, that's not it. She was more than that. Pretty, optimistic, she made things brighter. I even thought about asking Dad if I could make her mine." I've opened the box I keep locked inside me, the one where grief and anger swirl around each other relentlessly. "When she went missing, I lost it. Remember?" I stand and stagger to the kitchen and grab another bottle. "That's when this shit started. The drinking."

I plop back in the same spot, and Felix jumps over to me and curls up in my lap. "I figure I'll keep it going till it kills me. Might as well, right?"

"My real name is Georgia." Her whisper grazes my ear as she snuggles against me.

"That's a pretty name."

She laughs lightly. "Thanks. I thought maybe you'd prefer Mary."

I pull her closer. "You aren't a Mary. You're much more of a Georgia."

"You're definitely a Noah." She kisses my neck.

"Yeah?"

"You rescued Felix the stray, and you have a lizard. Come on. You've got a soft spot for animals."

"I didn't lead them two-by-two and save them from a flood."

"Maybe you will one day." Her voice softens, sleep invading. "I think you'll save lots of lives. Just give yourself a chance."

I pull the blanket up around us and dread the moment when I have to leave her here at the Cloister. She already sports too many bruises for my tastes, and I've spoken to Grace about it, who just brushes me off.

"I have to go." I slide out from the covers and dress.

She rolls onto her side and watches me with big blue eyes. "Hate to see you go, love to see you walk away."

I grin and drop one more kiss on her lips before leaving.

"She was beautiful," I whisper. "I'd never cared about a Maiden until her. Never took a real interest. I was going through the motions until that night I saw her at the bonfire." I toss the bottle cap onto the ottoman and take a drink. "Tequila. Damn." It still burns, so I need to drink more.

I lay my head back on the cushion and close my eyes. I'm too tired to talk to myself anymore, and I'm certain Felix is happy for the silence.

Mom killed Georgia. The thought eats through my brain like a worm. My eyes well. And here, in the safety of my place, I let the tears flow. Felix doesn't mind. Vengeance burns inside me, but the bond I have with my mother is still there. I hate her for killing Georgia. I take a drink at the thought. But I have to hold onto something. If I don't, I'll go upstairs and blow my fucking brains out. So I hold onto the hope that Mom can get us out of this mess, can free us from our father and offer a new way forward.

If she can't... I toss the bottle and it shatters against the front windows. Felix jumps and runs. If she can't, or if this is just a power play like Adam says, I'll make her answer for what she did to Georgia.

CHAPTER 27

"You'll be in the TV room today. Senator Roberts forwarded some videos he thinks you'll find instructional, and I have some business to attend to in Birmingham." Miriam flicks the projector on with easy precision. "Enjoy."

The screen flickers, and she disappears out the door at the back of the room.

I consider napping through the video, but quickly realize that's not an option as the first set of images appear. A woman is bent over a table, her hands bound behind her back, a gag in her mouth, and her legs apart, the ankles taped to the legs of the table. Her eyes plead with the camera.

A man appears behind her. He's wearing a black mask and nothing else. When he runs a hand down her back, she struggles and screams against the gag.

He laughs and motions for the cameraman to come

around to his side of the table. Shaky, the camera refocuses on her backside.

The man in the mask smears lube all over her, then shoves his hard cock into her ass. She screams again as blood wells around his shaft, but he doesn't stop.

I tell myself it's all for show, that it's porn, that she's just an actress. But the blood is too real, just like her anguished screams.

He grunts as he fucks her, the table screeching across the concrete floor with each animal thrust. The camera zooms in and out on her bloodied body. The masked man pulls out and moves around to her face.

He yanks her gag away.

"Please, let me go! Help!" she screams.

Everything inside me goes cold. She's not acting. It's real. All of it is real. Evan is sending me a message, a promise of things to come. It won't be her on the table once Evan has me in his clutches. It will be me.

She screams again, but the masked man slaps her hard across the face. "No one can hear you, slut." He shoves his cock into her mouth as another man appears, also nude except for his mask. He takes the spot between her bound legs, pounding hard into her as she gags on the first man's cock.

The camera pans out and shows a line of men, each of them wearing masks, each of them stroking themselves and waiting for their turn with the captive. Then the cameraman turns the lens around and focuses on himself. Senator Roberts' all-American grin fills the screen.

Bile rises in my throat, and I would vomit if I had any

food left in my stomach. I jump to my feet and run toward the projector. With a hard shove, I push it to the ground. It cracks and breaks against the wood floor, the light from the back of the room going dark, but the sound continues. The men grunting, some laughing, and her choking noises. I can't reach the speakers in the wall, can't do anything to stop the horror.

I turn and run, pushing out the door into the hallway. Then I stop. I expected to find a Spinner waiting outside. But there's no one. Just a long, empty hall to my left and my right.

My fight or flight turns into something more clever, and I take a left, creeping softly toward the kitchen. Most of the Spinners must be in training with the other Maidens, because the corridor is noticeably empty. The faint smell of vegetables roasting floats through the air, not the least bit appetizing.

Once I reach the kitchen, I crack the door and peek inside. Abigail stands in front of a large sink and washes dishes, the hiss of the sprayer covering any sound I might make. I can't see Chastity through the sliver. It's a risk, but I'm already in trouble for the projector, so I push the door open farther and glance to the right. Her back to me, Chastity is setting up the plates for lunch on the stainless steel table beneath the pass-through window.

I can't get her attention without catching Abigail's as well, so I gently close the door, then hurry to the dining room. I slip inside and keep to the shadowy wall, easing closer to the bright pass-through. When I get near enough, I make a "psst" noise.

Chastity's head pops up, her gaze scouring the dim dining room. "Who's there?"

"It's Delilah. Just keep working." The video will have seen me, but it doesn't have to show Chastity speaking with me. I'm in deep trouble, but I don't want her to join me there.

She drops her attention back to the plates and trays. "What are you doing?"

"I was in the TV room and got out. Can you tell me more about Georgia?"

She turns, likely checking to make sure Abigail's still busy.

Chastity keeps her voice so low I can barely hear it. "The Prophet didn't kill her."

"Who did?"

"I don't know. But the night she went missing, the Prophet was at the Cathedral for the birth of one of his sons. We think she was killed that night."

"Who is 'we'?" I scoot a little closer, hunching beneath the window.

"I can't put the others at risk by naming them, but there are women here who are willing to go to war if it comes to it. We just need an opening."

War? I was thinking that she had friends—maybe at the Chapel—who wanted to escape. Maybe Chastity and I have even more in common than I thought.

I let the truth out. "I want to bring it all down."

"It's the only way," she replies quickly.

"Who do you suspect killed Georgia?"

"That night, Noah and—"

The hiss of the water in the background stops. I hold my breath.

"Heavens, if we have to serve this broccoli one more time, I think the Maidens might revolt." Abigail shuffles some plates and pans, then the water turns back on.

"It was Noah?"

"Maybe." She slaps another tray onto the sill. "You have to go. Another Spinner will be coming any second to set up the dining room."

"Listen." I take a risk, and I hope it's worth it. "Tuesday. At the Temple. Can you make sure you go with the other Spinners that night?"

"Why?"

"Can you go?"

She slides some trays onto the window sill. "I can try. What's going to happen at—"

The water shuts off again. "All done here. I'm going to sit down and rest my tired old bones."

"Sounds good." Chastity's voice rises to a normal level. "I've got all these ready."

"Good deal." Abigail sighs along with the creak of a chair. "That's better." She's too close now. I can't say a word or she'll hear me.

I edge back toward the door.

I'm almost there when it swings open and the light flicks on.

CHAPTER 28

ADAM

"*I* heard you were a bad girl today." I toss my jacket on the foot of Delilah's bed and sit in front of her.

She looks up, defiance in her eyes. "No, not really."

Her biting tone makes me hard, because I'm a sick man who needs every ounce of pushback she gives me. "So, you *didn't* break the projector and you didn't go to the dining room looking for snacks and you didn't threaten the Spinner who caught you?"

She shrugs, her bare breasts jiggling slightly with the movement. "Maybe."

I laugh. She's fucking adorable. Even if this is a charade. Even if we have an intense, whispered conversation right around the corner. This playful, sharp edge of hers is still the real her, the one that captured my attention from the very start. I want to tell her I love it—her sass and her fire—but that's not a word I get to utter. Not to her. I don't deserve it.

"Did they send you to discipline me?"

"You do have a lot to learn." I lean back on my elbows. "Up."

She stands.

"Straddle me. I want to feel the heat of your cunt on my cock."

The knock on the door throws me out of my head-space—the only one I want to be in.

"What?" I shout.

"It's me." Noah's voice passes through the wood.

"Shit." I spent the better part of my day in Birmingham collecting drug money and enforcing agreements whenever necessary. I haven't had time to track him down and try to make him see my side.

"Who?" Delilah raises her eyebrows in question.

"Noah."

"Noah." Her voice hardens, and she stands, snatching her dress from the bed and throwing it over her head.

"What are you—"

She bolts to the door, opens it, and launches herself at him.

I rush after her.

Noah has her by the wrists, but she isn't giving up, screaming and doing her damndest to break free.

"Hey!" I grab her around the waist and wrench her back, but it's like trying to hold a greased pig.

She flails and manages to scratch Noah's face before I subdue her and drag her back into her room.

"What the fuck is going on?" My yell overcomes even her shrieks.

"He did it. He—" She lunges again, but I have her tightly in my grip.

"What did you do to her?" I lock eyes with him, but he looks perplexed as he touches the scratches on his cheek.

"Nothing." He shakes his head. "What the fuck is wrong with her?"

"I know what you did!" She's still wild, doing her best to get to him.

Her violence and noise has dormitory doors flying open, Protectors in various states of undress walking out as their Maidens peer from behind them.

"Noah, get in here." I drag Delilah backwards until we're in her bathroom.

Noah closes the hall door and follows, but he eyes her warily.

"I need you to calm down for just a minute and let me sort this out. Can you do that?" I talk in her ear.

She doesn't respond, her body still tense.

"Delilah, please." I release my hold just a bit, giving her room to breathe.

"Fine," she bites out.

"In here?" Noah peeks into the bathroom. "No way. She'll rip my face off."

I reach over and flip on the shower, then open the sink faucets so the room fills with the sound of running water.

Delilah doesn't move and lets me hold her again.

"Come in. She's calm."

Noah doesn't look convinced and runs a hand

through his hair before following my instructions and walking in, shutting the door behind them and then leaning against it, as far from her as possible.

"What the hell is going on?" I keep my voice even with the noise of the water. "Delilah?"

"Nothing."

I spin her around and force her gaze up to mine with a tilt of her chin. "Trust, little lamb. Not lies. Now tell me what is wrong."

Her eyes are gray marble, hard and unflinching. "He knows what he did."

I meet Noah's gaze over her crown. He throws his hands up and shakes his head, then mouths *I didn't do shit.*

"Okay, but *I* don't know what he did." I refocus on her. "So you'll have to tell me."

"No."

"Delilah." I glower. "You need to tell me. I can't fix it if I don't—"

The outer door swings open so hard it slams into the wall, and then someone's beating on the bathroom door.

"Get out here. Prophet wants to see you and Noah. Now!" It's Gray, followed by some unintelligible squawking from Grace.

"Shit." I stare at my obstinate Maiden as Noah keeps shaking his head.

"I said now!" Gray bangs on the door.

"We'll continue this later. For the moment, Noah, open the door." I push Delilah behind me, pinning her between the toilet and the wall.

Noah swings the door open and steps outside. Gray is red in the face, and a few other Protectors mill about in the main dormitory hall.

Gray reaches for my arm.

I glare at him. "Don't fucking touch me."

He drops his hand.

The crowd in the hall parts as I walk past and into the main Cloister corridor. Noah is at my back. We don't speak until we're out into the rainy night, the droplets pattering on the road and through the trees.

"You drive?" he asks.

I point to my car, and we both head for it. Questions pile up as I sit and start the engine, but I don't ask him anything. He already made his choice last night. Maybe I was a fool to think I could change his mind earlier. Then again, he did come to Delilah's room—presumably to speak to me.

He turns the radio up and clears his throat as I aim the car toward the main house.

"Look, I know you want to save her, okay?" He holds a hand out, palm up, as if reiterating that he's saying something utterly reasonable. "I can see why. And I know she's different for you. The way she looks at you. The way you've been acting ever since she got here. I get it. She's different. I know what that feels like."

"Where are you going with this?" I don't mean to say it as gruffly as I do.

"Well." He drops his hand. "Maybe we can get a message to Mom, you know? Maybe we can see if she can do something to keep Delilah away from that senator guy?"

"There's nothing she can do."

"You don't know that."

"I won't risk Delilah on a hazy guess of what Mom can or can't do. Not to mention the fact that being here, being married to Dad, has driven her batshit crazy."

"Don't say that." He faces me. "Don't talk about her that way."

"I don't want to, trust me." I slow as we approach the house. "But I need you to understand that Mom's vision for Heavenly is never going to come to life. Never. And I can't entrust Delilah to her."

"Do you love her?"

"Mom? Yeah."

He shakes his head. "You know who I mean."

I sigh and slow to a stop next to a set of golf carts parked at the rear of the house. "I can't answer that." *A lie.* I kill the engine but leave the radio on.

"So you're still dead set on throwing away your real family for a girl that you don't even know if you love?"

"What did you do to her?"

He doesn't catch the subject change, and answers, "I didn't do a thing. I have no clue what the fuck all that was."

"You swear you don't know?" I look into his eyes, needing the truth from him. If he's innocent of whatever she thinks he did, I should be able to work this out.

"I swear on Mom that I haven't done anything and don't know what she's talking about." He holds up his hand like he's swearing on a Bible instead of an old woman driven mad by grief and captivity.

"I believe you." I open my car door, but he grabs my arm.

"I meant what I said about Tuesday. We can't do it. We need to give Mom a chance." He lets go. "But I'm sorry about how it went down."

I sigh. "I'm sorry, too. And you need to change your mind."

"I won't." He gets out, and we slam our doors.

"We aren't done here." I stride to the back door.

He mumbles something. I ignore it and climb the staircase to the main floor.

"Boys! Get in here!" my father yells as soon as I swing the door open to the foyer.

"What are we going to tell him?" Noah whispers.

"Just tell him you grabbed her or something, made advances." I shrug. "And that's why she's pissed."

"Okay."

We stride in and sit down as Dad watches a replay of Delilah trying to take Noah's head off. I smirk. When she gets wound up, she fights like a banshee. It's fucking hot.

"What the hell is going on with you two?" My father slams a hand on his desk.

"I made a pass at her, and she's mad," Noah blurts.

Jesus. I want to slap him on the back of the head.

My father pinches the bridge of his nose. "Why would you make a pass at another Protector's Maiden?"

Noah shrugs. "She just, you know ... She's really pretty and, um, I like her ass."

"That's not like you." He narrows his eyes.

Noah shrugs. "Just something about her, I guess."

"What is it with this girl? First the senator and now you?" His demeanor changes to bemused and he pulls a cigar from his desk. "Maybe I should've charged more for her, huh?"

"You would have gotten it." I lean back in my chair.

"I think I may have." He lights up. "I do indeed. What about you, Adam? You seem to have taken a shine to her, too. I see you in her room, cuddling her instead of fucking her in the ass."

I shrug. "She's a fun little toy. I may as well spoil her a bit before Evan gets his hands on her. That's not going to be a picnic." Keeping my tone nonchalant has never been harder. Fuck, I want to kill that goddamn senator right along with my father.

He laughs, the sound scratching across my consciousness. "You got that right. He gets into some shit that even makes me blush. She's going to be in for a whole new world of pain as soon as she walks out those doors with him." He takes a big puff. "But she seems to cause a lot of trouble, that one. Maybe it'll be good to get rid of her. Especially since she'll be off our hands even sooner than I thought."

"What?" I dig my fingers into the arms of the chair.

"Oh, Evan is back from D.C." He takes another puff. "Going to come claim her at lunchtime tomorrow."

CHAPTER 29

DELILAH

*A*nother morning spent with Miriam almost has me wishing for the tortures of the training room. Instead, I learn all about Evan Roberts—his likes and dislikes, how he prefers his steak, who his parents are, what his siblings do, and how to be the best sex slave to him I can be.

Once she's done with me, I head to the dining room and take care to sit away from the other Maidens. No one else needs to suffer because of me. I'm halfway through what Abigail calls a "salad"—just lettuce with carrots and no dressing—when Grace walks in and points at me.

Damn. I can't seem to catch a break. I rise and follow her into the hallway.

"Go dress in your room. The senator has returned early and is here to claim you."

I must have misheard. That's the only explanation. "That's not right."

"Go." She crosses her arms over her stomach, a

feline smile on her lips. "He'll want to fuck you as soon as he gets his hands on you, I'm sure. There'll be so much blood." She claps like she just heard a juicy secret.

My stomach drops as reality caves in around me. "It's only Saturday. He's not supposed to be here till—"

"Go change." She bites out the words and shoves me toward the dormitories.

Hot tears well in my eyes as I walk down the corridor. It's over. My search for Georgia, my time with Adam. All over, and nothing to stop it.

"Hurry up." Grace stands at the dormitory entrance. "I can't wait to be rid of you."

Tears overflow and run down my cheeks as I sag against my door. No one can save me from this—not Adam and not me. I'm trapped. I have no doubt Evan has some horrible things planned for me the second he gets me alone.

Everything Adam planned for Tuesday—even if he goes through with it, it'll be too late for me. A wail rockets up from my lungs, and I press my forehead against the door.

"While this is entertaining, you're wasting my time." Grace slams her baton into the door next to my head. "Go."

I turn and scream at her. "Can you just be a human for two fucking seconds?"

She jabs the baton into my stomach, and I double over.

"Take that as a little parting gift from me to you, you

albino piece of trash," she hisses next to my ear, then shoves me against the door. "Go, before I hit you again."

I straighten up, the pain in my gut radiating through my abdomen. Coughing, I turn the knob and hobble away from her, closing the door behind me.

My eyes widen as Adam strides from the bathroom with a wooden chair in his hand and flips the lock over.

"What's wrong?" He furrows his brow. "Are you hurt?"

"No, I..." I straighten, the pain lessening as my confusion increases. "What are you doing?"

He wedges the chair under the door handle. "On the bed. Fast."

"What's going on? Grace said—" My throat closes up, a sob threatening, but I force the words out. "She said the senator is here for me."

"I've thought all night—all fucking night—of some way out of this. I only found one. This is my only choice." His steely determination tells me it's a bad choice, the outcomes unimaginable.

I have to stop this. All of it. My mind screams that there has to be some other way, but my heart sinks deeper into despair. "Adam."

"Take the dress off." He strips his shirt over his head.

"Adam." I press my hand to his warm chest. "What are you doing?"

"Saving you." He unfastens his belt and his jeans. "Hurry."

Everything becomes clear. He wants to make it official, to claim me and spoil me for any other man. That's how this fucked up world works—my only worth between my thighs—and he's playing the only card he has left. Ruining me to save me.

The thing is, he already ruined me for anyone else the moment he chose me at the bonfire.

"If you do this, what will happen to you?" I pull my dress over my head and toss it to the floor.

He shucks his jeans, his cock hard and ready. "I don't care. I just need them to see it, to know I've taken it."

"It was always yours." I kiss him, and he lifts me up and carries me to the bed. His mouth is rough, the urgency making him even more aggressive. I melt for him even now—even when what we're about to do may be a death sentence for both of us.

He prowls between my legs and takes a handful of my hair. "This is going to hurt."

"Wait." I shake my head. "What will they do to you? You have to tell me."

"I don't know." He kisses me again, hard and full of so much emotion that I'm overwhelmed and cling to him.

I force my mouth away from his. "I don't want to do this if it means they'll kill you. Will they?"

"I'd rather die than let you go to him." He presses his forehead to mine. "He bragged about what he intends for you. I heard every word the last time he was here. I won't let you go through that."

"Why won't you answer me? Will they kill you?" I struggle in his hold. "This can't be the only choice. There must be some other way."

"There isn't, little lamb. Do you trust me?" He kisses me again, his tongue asserting ownership.

When he lets up, I breathe out a yes. "But I don't want you to—"

"I'm sorry." He slaps a hand over my mouth and thrusts hard, seating himself deep inside me without warning.

His palm catches my cry, and he thrusts hard again. Searing heat cuts through me, and I know he's drawn blood. Rough and hard, he makes me his. No one could miss what's going on, could mistake what we're doing for anything other than what it is—a brutal claiming.

"I'm sorry," he whispers again and releases his hold on my mouth.

I kiss him through my tears and wrap my arms around his neck. He slows his harsh pace, loving me instead of fucking me. I relax, the pain fading as he moves in and out, hypnotic like the ocean. My hips surge up to his rhythm, meeting him stroke for stroke.

Even now, he can twist me until I'm drawn tight, my body needing a release that only he can give. He picks up his pace as someone starts beating on the door.

Grace yells his name.

"Ignore that. Look at me. Only me." He slides his hand between us and strokes my clit.

I hold eye contact, our communion deeper than it ever has been. Two souls entwined around each other as we leap over the edge.

More voices add to Grace's, men this time, and

someone starts pounding against the door so hard the light overhead flickers.

"Only me, Delilah." He kisses me again. "Only me."

"Emily." I stroke a hand down his cheek as my body begins to let go. "Call me Emily."

"My Emily." He strokes me faster, and I fall, my body clenching around him as I call out his name. He thrusts deep and grunts, masculine and perfect as his cock kicks inside me, coating me with him. My orgasm rolls over and over, and he kisses me again.

"I love you, Emily," he whispers against my lips. "Please remember that I love you, no matter what happens."

He doesn't give me a chance to say it back, just takes my lips in a searing kiss, and keeps kissing me until the door splinters and the Protectors rush in.

We only break contact when they yank him off me and drag him away. I scream and try to reach for him, but a Protector throws me on the bed and backhands me. The pain shocks me, and I get my last glimpse of Adam through watery eyes.

"Don't move, slut." The Protector glowers at me with cruel eyes as the rest of them follow Adam into the main hall.

He doesn't yell, even when I hear impacts of skin on skin. They're hurting him, maybe killing him.

"Stop!" I try to dart past the Protector again, but he grabs me by the hair and shoves me face first onto the bed.

"I may as well have a go since you're already ruined."

His hot breath burns my neck and I struggle, fighting against his hold on my hair.

"Get off me!"

A pained groan sounds from the hall, and I know in my bones that it's Adam.

"Stay still, whore." The Protector shoves me down harder and tries to push my knees apart.

"That's enough!" Chastity's voice breaks through the noise.

"Bitch, you don't tell me when it's enough." The Protector lets me go and grabs Chastity, slamming her against the wall. "Or do you want the same treatment as this whore over here?"

"Zion!" The Prophet's voice booms through the room, and Zion releases Chastity.

"Sir?"

"Bring the girl to the house." He points at me.

"Yes, sir."

"Do not touch her, understand? There may still be some value in her." He grimaces at me, then turns to the beating in the hall. "Take him to the Rectory."

"Yes, sir."

Chastity darts away from the wall and picks up my dress, then helps me get it on. Zion eyes us, but waits outside the room.

"What's going to happen?" My voice is small and shaky, and I try to get a glimpse of what's going on in the hall. There's too many bodies blocking my view.

Chastity's fingers tremble as she tucks my hair behind my ears. "I don't know."

"Will he kill Adam?" I can't stop the sob that bursts out on his name.

"Whatever happens, we'll deal with it." She kisses my forehead. "We're on the verge of something. I can feel it."

"What do you mean?"

"You have friends, Delilah. Remember that." She turns me and guides me into the hall toward Zion. "She's ready."

I cover my mouth when I see the blood on the floor, and the marks showing where they dragged him away.

"Come on." Zion grabs my elbow and hauls me to the rear door.

Another Protector already holds it open for us, and Zion walks me through and shoves me into the passenger seat of a golf cart. The sun is bright overhead, but no warmth reaches me. I peer through the trees for any sign of Adam, but he's gone, taken to the same pit where I suffered. Zion speeds up the hill and through the compound to the main house. The Prophet is already walking in as we drive up.

"Out." He walks around and pulls me with him into the house and up the steps.

He jerks his chin at the Prophet's bodyguard. "Where do you want her?"

He points to the same sitting room with the piano. "There."

Shouting echoes through the two-story foyer as Zion shoves me into the sitting room and slams the door. I collapse on the nearest couch and let my tears flow. There's no end to them. I berate myself, wondering if I could have stopped Adam, if I could have found some other way. But nothing comes to mind, no matter how hard I try. Maybe I should have just accepted my fate and gone with the senator.

I sob into the arm of the sofa. *You're weak, Emily. So fucking weak. You let him sacrifice himself for you. And now they're going to kill him.* I wish I could tell the voice to shut up, but I'm too afraid it's all true.

The door bursts open, and I push back into the arm of the sofa.

Evan rushes toward me, his face red.

"No!" I try to get up, but he slams me back down and holds me by my throat.

"Whore!" he shouts in my face and lifts my dress with his other hand.

I scratch him as he presses his hand between my thighs then yanks it back and stands.

His fingers come away pink and wet. He sniffs them, then scowls and pulls out a handkerchief, wiping his hand clean, then tossing the fabric on the floor. "You would have been the wife of a senator. Everything you ever wanted, I would have given you." He spits at my feet. "Now you're just a piece of trash."

The Prophet rushes in behind him. "Now, Evan. I think you've got the wrong idea. My son forced her. She would never have agreed to—"

"I don't give a shit *how* he did it," he barks. "He fucked her right out from under me. Took her virginity when I was signing the goddamn check."

The Prophet adopts an equitable tone. "Oh, come now, Evan. That doesn't mean you can't have her."

"She came for *him*." He spits again, his saliva slapping against the shiny wood floor next to my feet. "I don't buy damaged goods."

"Of course you do." The Prophet moves closer, his shrewd eyes assessing Evan. "You just don't pay full price." He hovers even nearer. "Look at her, Evan. Just look. Where will you ever find another one like her? You won't. She's still ready for whatever you want, ready to be bred. Nothing will come of this one violation; she's on the injections. For your purposes, she's still very much intact."

Evan's color is fading back to normal, but rage still burns in his eyes. "I'm not making any decisions today. I'm leaving."

"Evan, please—"

He strides past the Prophet. "I've been insulted enough for one day. I need to cool off."

The Prophet follows him into the foyer, their voices fading. "Might I send over some ladies from the Chapel to ease you?"

More footsteps approach, and I shrink back against the couch and pull my knees to my chest.

Noah stops in the doorway, his face cast in shadow as he watches me. He sighs, the sound almost as heavy as my guilt. "I hope you were worth it."

CHAPTER 30

ADAM

A harsh slap wakes me, but I can't see who laid the blow on my swollen cheek. It's too dark in the Rectory. Am I in the same room where they kept Delilah? *Emily,* her sweet voice reminds me gently. *My name is Emily.*

"Wake up, *pendejo.*" Castro smacks me again, whipping my head to the side.

"Fuck you." My voice is a croak. Someone managed to get a decent throat punch in at the Cloister, and I've been tasting blood on my breath ever since.

He unlocks the shackles holding me upright against the metal frame of a box spring. "Should have listened. Should have stayed in line."

I spit in his face, and he hits me again, the shock to my jaw adding to the rest of the pain pulsing through me.

He drags me from the small, gloomy room into a dim corridor. The room at the end is bright, and I squint as we get closer. Tossing me inside, he stands in the doorframe, his hand on the semiautomatic rifle slung across his shoulders. I don't know why he's so worried. At least one of my ribs is broken, my left arm likely out of the socket. I couldn't do a thing to him, though it pleases me he's still worried.

"Son." My father sits in a regal chair—far too swank for this filthy prison. But, as always, he loves to stand out.

"That's me." I drag myself into a sitting position and lean against the chilly cinderblock wall.

He frowns as he looks over my nude, battered form. Maybe he isn't satisfied with the damage that's been done.

"You broke the rule with Grace before, when you were younger and dumber. But I thought that having to watch your bastard child die would be enough of a punishment to get you in line."

"Don't talk about her!" I try to rise up onto my knees, but my body won't cooperate, I flop back down and scrape my bare skin along the harsh gray wall. Useless.

"I don't say this to hurt you." He opens his palms, a benevolent light in his eye. Even now, he keeps the charade going. "I say it to remind you that I've given you opportunities to change your ways, to follow me and become a truly devoted follower of the Lord and the Father of Fire. I thought that the winter solstice would be your time to prove yourself." He sighs and leans back, scrubbing a hand down his face. "But you still don't believe. You refuse to obey me. You deliberately break my law." His ire rises, his face reddening, but he tamps it down. "And you did it right in front of me, flouting your disobedience."

"I'll never be obedient to a monster like you." I spit a wad of blood on the threadbare rug. "And I won't rest until the day you burn in hell."

"Why, son?" He seems genuinely puzzled, his graying brows drawing together. "Why do you have such hate in your heart for me? I know I've been hard on you. I know things were different between us once I received my mission from the Father of Fire. I've spoken to you in cruel ways and not given you the due you're owed as my firstborn. But these small injuries surely couldn't have created such a foul, disobedient son."

I laugh, my lips splitting along fresh seams. "Why? Why do I want you dead? I can think of a million reasons. But there's only one that signed your death warrant. Just one."

He frowns.

"Faith." I hate to say her name in this rotten place, but nothing can tarnish her. Not anymore.

"You could have other children, but you've refused to wed." He shrugs, as if replacing Faith is something as simple as plucking another child from out of thin air. "All that could have been remedied. But now, we're past that. You've finally gone too far. Hurting me, hurting Heavenly—"

"Are you going to torture me? Then get on with it. I'd much prefer it to you talking me to death."

"Even now, you thumb your nose at the man who gave you life." He shakes his head. "'A son honors his father, and a slave his master. If I am a father, where is the honor due me?'"

"No one quotes scripture better than the devil."

"'I will give you all their authority and splendor; it has been given to me, and I can give it to anyone I want to. If you worship me, it will all be yours.'"

I shake my head, even though something creaks perilously in my neck. "Now you've skipped straight to quoting the devil himself."

"The Father of Fire's words are still true, Adam. I worship him, and he has given me so many blessings. You could have those blessings, too, if you would only worship me as your Prophet and the Father of Fire as your god."

Blood pools in my mouth as I glare at him.

"But you're obstinate and willful." He hardens, his dark eyes narrowing on me. "I've spared the rod for too long. You—"

"The whippings weren't enough, huh?" I laugh, bloody spit running down my chin. "Can't beat the devil into me, so I guess it's time to move on to bigger and better. You going to tickle my feet till I squeal? Maybe have Castro over there take a feather to my balls? Or maybe you'd rather do that yourself?"

He jerks forward and grabs my hair, yanking me to him as he leans down. "I know you think this bravado is fooling me. It's not, son. Maybe you even think the stunt you pulled with your Maiden will save her from Senator Roberts. Is that it?"

"Fuck you."

"It won't save her. He's too invested in her now. He'll

buy her—paying far less of course—and then he'll take out all the anger he feels toward you on her." He adopts a concerned mask. "He'll hurt her in ways she can't even imagine. All because of you. I'll make sure of it, build his rage up until he won't be able to help himself. He won't even make it off the compound before he rapes her. I'm certain of it. But then, I saw the video. She's a wanton little slut, isn't she? It won't be rape at all. She's cock-hungry. Your mistake was in thinking she only had an appetite for yours. She—"

I throw my head forward as hard as I can.

He yells and releases me, then puts a hand to his bloodied nose. "Castro!"

The impact reverberates through me, amplifying every bit of pain in my face. Then the butt of Castro's gun comes out of nowhere, and the world goes black.

CHAPTER 31

DELILAH

The drive to the Cathedral is shrouded in night, and I cower in the back seat of the sedan as we roll through the compound. Noah sits next to me but doesn't look at me as one of the other Protectors drives.

We turn off onto a narrow road through the trees and check with a guard before continuing down the lane. I don't know what awaits me, and all I can think about is Adam.

"Where is he?" I whisper.

Noah stares straight ahead, his body tight. I hate him and despise him even more for his silence.

We pull up outside a stark white building almost as large as the sanctuary. Two guards stand at the wide front doors. My car door opens and a Protector yanks me up, then pushes me forward. I stumble and catch myself, but manage to make it to the doors. The nearest guard looks down his nose at me, but enters a code to let me in. I hesitate and glance at the woods.

"Don't even think about it." The Protector at my back shoves me forward into a new hell that gleams in shades of white and baby blue.

A large living room sprawls to my left, several couches strewn around along with children's toys in different areas on the light blue carpet. On my right, a huge dining area sparkles in the bright lights from overhead. Plenty of high chairs and round tables, as well as smaller tables for children, fill the space.

"Walk." The Protector stays on my heels as we follow the tile floor that separates the living and dining areas. Another set of doors is open just ahead, both of them pinned back against the wall.

I'm herded down a long corridor decorated with children's handprints and whimsical animals along the walls. Doors line the way, all of them closed, but windows show me sleeping children inside. I can't tell, but I know they must be the same ones from Sunday service—the same ones at the solstice ceremony.

Where is Adam? Here? I doubt it, but I hold onto that vain hope anyway.

We pass through more doors, and this time, the scent of baby lotion tinges the air. A Spinner holds a crying infant and dances back and forth in a nursery area to my right. There have to be at least a dozen babies in there.

"All the Prophet's?"

"Shut up." He shoves me again until we pass the nursery, then enter a wide open room.

Above, glass separates the inside from the night sky, square panes framing the inky blackness. The floor is carpeted in the same baby blue, and there are cushy couches and sitting areas here and there. A few women look up as we enter, whatever conversation they were having halting abruptly. They are barely dressed, as if negligees are standard issue, and regard me with open suspicion.

"New girl?" One stands, her dark hair in a long braid down her back.

"Temporary." The Protector pushes me down onto the nearest couch, then turns and leaves. When the doors shut behind him, some sort of pneumatic lock shoots into place.

"Name?" The one with the braid walks over and sits next to me, her green eyes perusing my face.

"Delilah."

"I'm Ruth." She doesn't shake, but gives me a small smile. "Looks like you've been thrown into the pit with the rest of us."

A pregnant woman waddles over and rests on a chair across from us. "Temporary? What does that even mean?"

Something catches my eye behind her. A side wall is arranged with several of the same implements from the training room, along with many others I can't name. A bench sits to one side, the same sort of "horse" I've been on at the Cloister. A chill shoots through me, and my mouth goes dry.

I turn back to the one with the long braid. "I need to get out of here."

She laughs, but it's not mean—not like what I'm used

253

to from Grace. "If you find a way, be sure to tell the rest of us."

More women creep out from the alcoves along the walls, their eyes bleary with sleep as they inspect the new arrival.

"That's blasphemy, Ruth." The pregnant one stands and waddles away. "We are safe here with the Prophet."

Ruth ignores her and leans closer. "So, what are you in for?"

"I have to get out. He's going to hurt Adam. Maybe kill him. I don't know. He's at the Rectory, I think. But—"

"Adam?" She cocks her head to the side. "His son Adam?"

"Yes." Can't she hear the urgency in my voice? "But I need to get to him. Now."

"And do what?" She lets her gaze stray down my body. "What's your plan? You're a white waif. What can you do to a dozen armed men, maybe more?"

"I don't know." I grab my hair and pull it, as if the pain will grant me some clarity. All it gives me is a headache. "I just have to get to him."

"There are guards here constantly. On all the doors. Watching at all times. There's no way out unless the Prophet wants you out."

"No!" I stand and sprint to the door, banging on it even though I know it's useless. "Let me out!"

"Shh!" a woman nearby hisses. "You'll wake the babies."

I bang some more until my arms tire and I slide to the floor, my tears coming in a torrent of frustration.

"Let me out," I whisper over and over until my voice is gone.

Ruth walks over to me and offers her hand. "Come on, Maiden. That won't do any good."

"I have to—" My breath catches, and I take several small inhales. The room spins.

"You're hyperventilating." She kneels next to me. "Just breathe slowly. Big breaths. Try to hold them a little."

"I can't."

"You can. You have to calm down." She moves closer, her eyes holding mine. "Chastity told me about you," she whispers.

I finally catch my breath and take in huge gulps of air. "You're one of—"

"Shh." She presses a finger to her lips, her eyes wide with warning. "Not now. Come with me and get cleaned up. There's nothing we can do but wait."

"Wait?" I can't bear the seconds since he's been ripped away from me. Adding more to them is a death sentence.

"Wait." She gives me a stark nod and pulls me to my feet.

"Everyone!" the guard yells as the women scramble to throw on their long dresses.

Ruth wouldn't give me any information last night, just told me over and over to wait and see. She eventually disappeared—perhaps to her bed in one of the alcoves. I tossed and turned on the couch, playing out one horrible scenario of Adam's punishment after the other until the sun began to peek through the glass panes above.

An alarm sounded about five minutes ago, and the entire room woke up, women hurrying to ready themselves.

"What's going on?" I dart over to Ruth when she appeared in the main area.

"Looks like we've been summoned. We're going out."

"Out? Is that normal?"

She glances at the glass ceiling. "At daybreak on a Sunday morning? No."

I don't like the sinking feeling that settles in my stomach. Something bad is coming. Will I survive it? "Do you know why?"

"Not sure." She fixes her hair into a messy braid and lines up at the main door. "Stick with me."

I stand next to her, and after a few minutes all the women are ready. The doors open, and we're greeted by the armed guards who walk us through the nursery and children's area. Some of the women wave and coo at their sleepy kids, but the young ones appear to be staying behind.

The outer doors open, and we're hustled into a waiting bus, the interior painted the same baby blue as inside the Cathedral. Ruth sits next to me, but offers no comfort. She's too busy watching everything, her gaze incisive and sweeping.

I press my shaking hands to my face and try to block

out the world, to sink into nothing. It doesn't work. I can hear the sounds of Adam being beaten, see the look in his eyes when they dragged him away from me.

"Oh, God." I sob into my palms. Everything is spinning out of control. What little hope I had is gone, nothing but ashes in its place.

We roll onto a rougher road, the gravel compacting beneath the tires. I look out from behind my hands to see the white bus from the Cloister and another red bus that I've noticed parked outside the Chapel.

"Gang's all here," Ruth deadpans as we pull to a stop.

"Out." The Protector at the front walks down the steps.

"I can't." I shake my head. "What's out there?"

"You have to." Ruth takes my hand and pulls me with her out into the cold morning. "And we'll find out."

My steps are stiff, my body aching from lack of sleep and too much tension. The Maidens are already standing in a semi-circle on one side of the clearing, the women from the Chapel on the other. I find Chastity in the Spinners, but her face gives nothing away. Two Protectors hold Noah off to the side, and his expression is a mix of hatred and fear. I wonder if I look the same, strained to the point of breaking. His mother is with him, but she only has the Prophet's bodyguard to keep her in place.

The women from the Cathedral form another semi-circle slightly apart from the other women. Two four-wheelers sit to the opposite side of the clearing near two crosses, and Protectors move around like ants in the area.

I peer in that direction, but I can't see anything for the men and machines in my way.

The Prophet stands in the very center, his hands in a furry muffler, a knit hat covering his head. A white butterfly plaster is spread across the bridge of his nose.

"My faithful." He smiles. "So beautiful this morning, all of you."

I can barely stand, and I lean on Ruth for support. She holds me up, her spine straight as I begin to fall apart.

"But we are here for some ugly business. One amongst us has committed a grievous sin against me. One that cannot be easily forgiven. Atonement is the order of the day." He adopts a more sober expression. "As the Lord said to Moses, 'Whoever has sinned against me I will blot out of my book.'" He pulls one hand from the muffler and holds it over his head, then closes his fingers into a fist.

A hard sound rockets through the air, followed by a deep cry of agony. Adam.

I know that sound—a hammer hitting a nail. My knees go, and I drop to the ground. The harsh sound comes again and again—each blow causing more wails. My tears overflow, and I don't know how I'm breathing. The noise stops for a moment, then starts again. I cover my ears, but I can still hear him, can still *feel* his torment twisting deep inside me.

"Please, stop! It was me!" I try to crawl to the Prophet, but rough hands pull me up and force me to stand witness.

"Shut up." A Protector wraps an arm around my middle and grips my throat with his cold palm.

When the hammer strokes are done, the Prophet lowers his hand. "'The Lord is slow to anger, abounding in love and forgiving sin and rebellion. Yet he does not leave the guilty unpunished.'" He scans the crowd, his gaze landing on me at the very last moment. "And nor do I." He walks forward as two men mount the four-wheelers.

The four-wheelers start up, then slowly move forward. A chain tightens behind them, and then I see it. Not two crosses, but three. Everything inside me freezes and cracks, and I don't blink, or breathe, or move.

Adam is nailed to the center one, his hands pierced with spikes, his arms bound to the wood with leather straps. The sun rises behind him, the light blinding as he's hoisted upright.

His roars of pain shatter the beauty of the new day, leaving nothing but horror in their wake.

ACKNOWLEDGMENTS

Thanks to Mr. Aaron for reading my pages with a feverish need to know what happens next. You're the best.

Thanks to Viv for doing the same, and with even more glee at rubbing it in that you got to read before almost anyone else. Your help is always invaluable.

Great work on catching all my errors, Stacey and Trina! Y'all are amazing and eagle-eyed.

I'm always grateful to Wander Aguiar for creating amazing images and to Perfect Pear for bringing my covers to life.

Thanks, readers, for sticking around and tromping through this dark, mysterious swamp with me. I couldn't do it without you.

The Church is coming next. Redemption is at hand for some, judgment for others, and death is always lurking.

Xx,
Celia

,

Dark Romance

Acquisition: The Complete Series

Darkness lurks in the heart of the Louisiana elite, and only one will be able to rule them as Sovereign. Sinclair Vinemont will compete for the title, and has acquired Stella Rousseau for that very purpose. Breaking her is part of the game. Loving her is the most dangerous play of all.

*includes Sinclair, Counsellor, Magnate, and Sovereign

Blackwood

I dig. It's what I do. I'll literally use a shovel to answer a question. Some answers, though, have been buried too deep for too long. But I'll find those, too. And I know where to dig—the Blackwood Estate on the edge of the Mississippi Delta. Garrett Blackwood is the only thing standing between me and the truth. A broken man—one with desires that dance in the darkest part of my soul—he's either my savior or my enemy. I'll dig until I find all his secrets. Then I'll run so he never finds mine. The only problem? He likes it when I run.

Dark Protector

From the moment I saw her through the window of her flower shop, something other than darkness took root inside me. Charlie shone like a beacon in a world that had long since lost any light. But she was never meant for me, a man that killed without remorse and collected bounties drenched in blood.

I thought staying away would keep her safe, would shield her from me. I was wrong. Danger followed in my wake like death at a slaughter house. I protected her from the threats that circled like black buzzards, kept her safe with kill after kill.

But everything comes with a price, especially second chances for a man like me.

Killing for her was easy. It was living for her that turned out to be the hard part.

Nate

I rescued Sabrina from a mafia bloodbath when she was

13. As the new head of the Philly syndicate, I sent her to the best schools to keep her as far away from the life--and me--as possible. It worked perfectly. Until she turned 18. Until she came home. Until I realized that the timid girl was gone and in her place lived a smart mouth and a body that demanded my attention. I promised myself I'd resist her, for her own good.

I lied.

The Bad Guy

My name is Sebastian Lindstrom, and I'm the villain of this story.

I've decided to lay myself bare. To tell the truth for once in my hollow life, no matter how dark it gets. And I can assure you, it will get so dark that you'll find yourself feeling around the blackened corners of my mind, seeking a door handle that isn't there.

Don't mistake this for a confession. I neither seek forgive-ness nor would I accept it. My sins are my own. They keep me company. Instead, this is the true tale of how I found her, how I stole her, and how I lost her.

She was a damsel, one who already had her white knight. But every fairy tale has a villain, someone waiting in the wings to rip it all down. A scoundrel who will set the world on fire if that means he gets what he wants.

That's me.

I'm the bad guy.

Contemporary Romance

You've Got Fail

She's driving me crazy. Or am I the one driving myself crazy? I can't tell anymore. Ever since Scarlet Rocket showed up in the flesh, she's turned my structured world upside down. My neatly ordered life, my hand-painted Aliens versus Vampires figurines, my expertly curated comics collection--none of these things provide any shelter from her sexy, sassy onslaught. It's a disaster of my own making. She didn't exist until I created her. Now, I can't get her out of my mind, and all I want to do is get her into my bed. Never mind that she's a thief, a liar, a con-woman. Every step she takes leaves chaos in her wake. And damn if I don't want more of it.

Kicked

Trent Carrington.
Trent Mr. Perfect-Has-Everyone-Fooled Carrington.
He's the star quarterback, university scholar, and happens to be the sexiest man I've ever seen. He shines at any angle, and especially under the Saturday night stadium lights where I watch him from the sidelines. But I know the real him, the one who broke my heart and pretended I didn't exist for the past two years.

I'm the third-string kicker, the only woman on the team and nothing better than a mascot. Until I'm not. Until I get my chance to earn a full scholarship and join the team as first-string. The only way I'll make the cut is to accept help from the one man I swore never to trust again. The problem is, with each stolen glance and lingering touch, I begin to realize that trusting Trent isn't the problem. It's that I can't trust myself when I'm around him.

Tempting Eden

A modern re-telling of Jane Eyre that will leave you breathless...

Jack England

Eden Rochester is a force. A whirlwind of intensity and thinly-veiled passion. Over the past few years, I've worked hard to avoid my passions, to lock them up so they can't harm me—or anyone else—again. But Eden Rochester ignites every emotion I have. Every glance from her sharp eyes and each teasing word from her indulgent lips adds more fuel to the fire. Resisting her? Impossible. From the moment I held her in my arms, I had to have her. But tempting her into opening up could cost me my job and much, much more.

Eden Rochester

When Jack England crosses my path and knocks me off my high horse, something begins to shift. Imperceptible at first, the change grows each time he looks into my eyes or brushes against my skin. He's my assistant, but everything about him calls to me, tempts me. And once I give in, he shows me who he really is—dominant, passionate, and with a dark past. After long days of work and several hot nights, I realize the two of us are bound together. But my secrets won't stay buried, and they cut like a knife.

Bad Bitch

Bad Bitch Series, Book 1

They call me the Bad Bitch. A lesser woman might get her panties in a twist over it, but me? I'm the one who does the twisting. Whether it's in the courtroom or in the bedroom, I've never let anyone - much less a man - get the upper hand.

Except for that jerk attorney Lincoln Granade. He's dark, mysterious, smoking hot and sexy as hell. He's nothing but a bad, bad boy playing the part of an up and coming premiere attorney. I'm not worried about losing in a head to head battle with this guy. But he gets me all hot and bothered in a way no man has ever done before. I don't like a person being under my skin this much. It makes me want to let go of all control, makes me want to give in. This dangerous man makes me want to submit to him completely, again, and again, and again...

Hardass

Bad Bitch Series, Book 2

I cave in to no one. My hardass exterior is what makes me one of the hottest defense lawyers around. It's why I'm the perfect guy to defend the notorious Bayou Butcher serial killer - and why I'll come out on top.

Except this new associate I've hired is unnaturally skilled at putting chinks in my well-constructed armor. Her brazen talk and fiery attitude make me want to take control of her and silence her - in ways that will keep both of us busy till dawn. She drives me absolutely 100% crazy, but I need her for this case. I need her in my bed. I need her to let loose the man within me who fights with rage and loves with scorching desire...

Total Dick

Bad Bitch Series, Book 3

I'm your classic skirt chaser. A womanizer. A total d*ck. My reputation is dirtier than a New Orleans street after a Mardi Gras parade. I take unwinnable cases and win them. Where people see defeat, I see a big fat paycheck. And when most men see rejection, it's because the sexiest woman at the bar has already promised to go home with me.

But Scarlett Carmichael is the one person I can't seem to conquer. This too-cool former debutante has it all—class, attitude, and a body that begs to be worshiped. I've never worked with a person like her before—hell, I've never played nice with anyone before in my life, and I'm not about to start with her. This woman wasn't meant to be played nicely with. It's going to be dirty. It's going to be hot. She's about to spend a lot of time with the biggest d*ck in town. And she's going to love every minute of it...

Fantasy Romance

Incubus

An incubus who feeds off the sexual desires of others, Roth de Lis has never been denied the pleasure of a woman's body...until now. Lilah, once a warrior maiden in the service of a goddess, languishes on earth after being cast out from the slopes of Mount Olympus.
Lilah will do anything to return home, including betraying Roth. As she spins her web of lies, Roth begins a slow, wicked seduction that eventually threatens to consume them both. But when Lilah's deceit comes to light, will their torrid love affair be able to overcome a pact with the darkest of gods?

The Reaper's Mate

This job. Boring is too colorful a word for it. I've been escorting humans to the afterlife for millennia. I'm over it. But when you're the son of the two greatest reapers of all time, reaping is in your blood. My latest appointment is with one Annabelle Lyric, a twenty-eight year old New Orleans party planner. Snoozefest. But there is one bonus to this assignment: it's Halloween night. In New Orleans. And she's attending a posh party whilst unaware of her impending demise. I've been tasked with taking Annabelle's soul right after the masked ball. The good news? I'll fit right in with all the costumed partygoers. The bad news? That hits me when I realize Annabelle is much more than my next victim, she's my fated mate.

Short Sexy Reads

THE HARD & DIRTY HOLIDAYS

A steamy series of holiday-inspired novellas that are sure to warm your heart and your bed.

A Stepbrother for Christmas
Bad Boy Valentine
Bad Boy Valentine Wedding
F*ck of the Irish
Christmas Candy

THE FORCED SERIES

These are just as filthy as they sound. Scorching stories of dubious consent, all with a satisfying twist.

Forced by the Kingpin
Forced by the Professor
Forced by the Hitmen
Forced by the Stepbrother
Forced by the Quarterback

THE SEXY DREADFULS

A series of erotica novellas starring Cash Remington. Not romance, but something hotter and a bit more risqué.

Cash Remington and the Missing Heiress
Cash Remington and the Rum Run

ABOUT THE AUTHOR

Celia Aaron is a recovering attorney and USA Today bestselling author who loves romance and erotic fiction. Dark to light, angsty to funny, real to fantasy—if it's hot and strikes her fancy, she writes it. Thanks for reading.

Sign up for my newsletter at celiaaaron.com to get information on new releases. (I would never spam you or sell your info, just send you book news and goodies sometimes). ;)

Stalk me:
www.celiaaaron.com

CPSIA information can be obtained
at www.ICGtesting.com
Printed in the USA
LVHW010851281018
595121LV00010B/640/P

9 781717 289827